Prologue

Quinn

Nothing in life prepares you for these moments... when your entire world starts crumbling around you.

Numbness. That's what I feel, that's actually all I feel. Like I have been going through the motions for the past week. A spectator looking in, unable to speak or make important decisions.

Empty.

I am a tough person. I've never really been one to wear my heart on my sleeve; I take what life throws at me, and I handle it like the boss that I am. But this? How do I even begin to handle this, when I can barely even understand it enough to accept that it's real? Some people say that everyone has a soulmate, yet some go their entire lives and never get to meet the one person that was truly made for them. Not me though, I met my soulmate in high school, and I've been completely captivated since.

Until now.

Up until a week ago, my entire life was planned out. I was supposed to marry the man of my dreams in just six short months. I look down at my finger that holds the perfect solitaire diamond ring.

"Quinn, sweetie, are you ready? We need to be there in thirty minutes." My mom's voice pulls me out of the monologue that has been on repeat for the past six days.

"Yeah mom, I will be right down."

My parents are just walking on eggshells around me. It's like they are waiting for me to cry or scream or show any emotion at all. But here I am, sitting in my childhood bedroom, furnished with the canopy bed, stuffed animals and pink walls that are still covered in boy band posters. I haven't forced myself to go home yet, the home that we shared, the home that just seven nights ago he walked out of, telling me that he would see me in seventy two hours. Instead, for the past week I have sat here, staring at these annoyingly happy pink walls, trying to prepare myself for the day that wasn't in my plans, in our plans.

The car ride to the funeral home is mostly silent, other than my mom making small talk about the weather and how warm it is for mid April in Michigan. My dad, he is trying. Trying to make me smile, or laugh, or show any type of emotion at all. But as much as he tries, he seems to come up short every time. So he just continues to glance back at me through the rearview mirror, as if he is making sure that I am not about to jump off some imaginary cliff on which I'm teetering.

Giving me his, "everything is going to be ok" smile he says "You look beautiful baby."

My breath catches in my throat.

I manage to whisper, "Thanks, Dad"

Baby... that's what Brett used to call me.

"Brett! Stop chasing me" I squeal. "What are we doing here anyway? You hate the beach." He always says, "why drive an hour to Lake Michigan when we live in a town surrounded by the state's most beautiful lakes."

"Because my baby loves the beach, so sometimes you just have to give the woman who owns your heart what she wants," he leans in and kisses me on the tip of my nose.

I feel my cheeks start to pink but I do a very obvious eye roll to try to hide it. How is it that after ten years this man still gives me butterflies?

"Well, aren't you Mr. Romantic." I gush as I try and pull him down into the sand.

"Oh no you don't," he says, pulling me back up to my feet. "Lets go walk the pier and look at all the boats coming in."

After forty minutes of hand holding, looking all the giant boats coming in off the lake, and sneaking in small kisses, we are back where we started. I get lost in admiring the different colors of the sun setting over the lake until a small noise grabs my attention. I turn back to Brett, only to find him on one knee.

"Quinn Rose Harris, I have been in love with you since we were fifteen years old. From the minute you walked into our Basic Econ class and sat down next to me with your bright green eyes and beautiful smile, I knew you were the one that I wanted to spend the rest of my life with." He reaches in his back pocket and pulls out the most beautiful princess cut diamond I have ever seen. Warmth and excitement explode throughout my body. I didn't even realize I was crying until I feel a tear fall and land on my trembling hands. "Quinn, baby, will you marry me, and make me the luckiest asshole in the world?"

His proposal is exactly what I would expect from him- short, simple, to the point, and perfect. For added dramatics I tap my chin like I am seriously considering saying no to the man whom I have loved for what seems like my entire life.

"Yes! Of course, I will marry you!" I giggle. He slides the ring onto my left hand, and it's a perfect fit. Just like the two of us.

We sit here, his arms and legs wrapped around me, watching the sunset across the lake, while talking and making plans for our future.

"Quinn, we are here. It's time to go inside." My Dad says, waking me from my memory.

A future. That's something we'll never have. He was supposed to be my happily ever after, and now he's gone.

The funeral is a blur, and before I can begin to grasp what's happening, I am watching my forever being lowered into the ground. Everyone around me is crying- my parents, Brett's parents, my best friend Halee, even the guys from the firehouse show signs of grief and pain. Why can't I? I just stand here, feeling numb and replaying the last eleven years of my life like my own personal slideshow.

Then it happens, the moment I have been dreading… the "Last Call".

The department tone goes off.

"Firefighter Rhodes to Central Dispatch. Firefighter Rhodes to Central Dispatch. Having heard no response, Firefighter Brett Rhodes has responded to his last call on earth. Rhodes has now become a Guardian who will help watch out for all others as they respond to emergencies. Brett Rhodes completed his tour as a Firefighter in this life. Rest peacefully until we meet again Rhodes, we got it from here… Central Dispatch clear at 13:00 hours."

Then, with the sound of the bagpipes, come all my tears.

Chapter 1

Quinn

One year later...

One year. It's hard to believe that a year ago today I watched them lower Brett into the ground. I can't even try to pretend I remember much of that day, because I don't. I read something once about the brain having this ability to block out tragic events to help with the healing process. Trust me when I say, it's complete shit. I may not have much recollection of events that took place on that terrible April day, but I can tell you, it doesn't make anything any easier. I still find myself falling asleep with my salty tears soaking the pillow, and wake to the smell of vodka on my breath.

They don't write books that tell you how to move on when the love of your life runs into a burning building to be a hero, only he doesn't make it back out. Trust me, I have checked. Everyone wants to help; they keep telling me it is going to be ok, or that it will get easier with time. And honestly, I am waiting... waiting for that morning when I wake up and I feel different. When maybe it doesn't feel like someone is ripping my heart out of my chest and setting it on fire with a blow torch. But that day hasn't come yet.

Today, I have to pull my shit together and pretend for the entire community that I am doing ok. Today the guys down at the department have organized an event in Brett's honor. All of the money raised will go towards education for current and future firefighters. Shit, he would have loved this. An entire night dedicated to him, his picture blown up on a banner, his face splattered on all of the brochures to be handed out, and an entire foundation created in his honor. Somewhere, he is sitting back with a beer in his hand and a gorgeous smile on his face because, even though he is no longer here, he is still making a difference.

My best friend Halee agreed to be my plus one for the night. I think that she assumes if she didn't physically come to pick me up, then I wouldn't show. But that is where she is wrong. There is no way that I would ever let Brett down like that, and that's exactly what me not going would do, disappoint him. I can't even think about how he would feel about my recent behavior anyways. Drinking was never something I enjoyed; when we would go out I was always the designated driver.

But these days, drinking is the only thing that seems to numb the pain.

I hear my front door open, "Quinn, I'm here. Are you about ready?" Speak of the devil. If Halee is anything, she is punctual. I look at myself one last time in the mirror, run my hands down the front of the black, knee-length dress, grab the strappy black heels off of the bed and head out towards the person who has been my anchor the last twelve months. Once I round the corner, Halee gasps, "Q, that dress was made for you! You. Are. Stunning."

"Thanks babe, you don't look half bad yourself. Is that new?" She nods and twirls, the turquoise dress she is wearing has a sweetheart neckline and is fitted to the waistline where it slightly flows down to about mid thigh. The color is perfect with her platinum blonde hair and baby blue eyes, "You will definitely be getting attention in that outfit tonight. I love it."

"Oh good. This just in- I am officially back on the market again as of…" she glances down at an imaginary watch on her wrist, "an hour ago."

We head out the door, and I turn to make sure I locked it up behind me. "What? What happened, Hales? You really seemed to like this one, what was his name, Jared?"

"Jeremy."

"Oh shit, I knew that. I am a terrible friend, sorry. I promise I really do listen to you when you are talking, his name just slipped my mind."

As we climb into her car, she lays her hand onto my arm. "Q, don't worry about it. You have had a lot going on. And sadly, he isn't even worth remembering."

"Want to talk about it?" I ask, hoping I can try to make up for the fact that I didn't even know this dudes name, and she had been seeing him for a few months. I really am a shitty friend.

"Not much to talk about. He was upset that I was coming to Brett's event with you. It worked him up so much he decided to call me a few choice names, so I told him I thought it was best we part ways. Ok, so maybe I didn't put it so nicely but whatever. Long story short, I am on the prowl again."

"Hales, I could have come to this alone, or with my parents, or hell, I could have third wheeled with you two. I am so sorry…"

She raises one hand from the steering wheel and without breaking eye contact with the road, says, "Stop. He didn't even know Brett. I'm pretty sure he was just wanting to come for the open bar. Plus, any man who can't understand that I need to be here for my girl tonight… well, he isn't someone I want in my life."

As we pull into the parking lot I suddenly feel like an elephant is sitting on my chest. Halee must have sensed it because she puts the car in park, turns to me, and pulls my face so we are eye to eye. "Quinn Harris, you are going to be fine. And for those moments when you aren't fine, I will be right there to hold your hand."

I let out a long deep breath. How did I get so lucky to have her? "Thank you, Hales. I love you."

"You too, girl, you too."

✄✄✄

"What can I get ya?" the older of the two men working behind the bar asks me.

"Um… I will take two vodka sodas please." I glance back around the room, checking to see if Halee is out of the bathroom yet. We barely made it through the door before I was bombarded with people and fake conversations. Each one the same as the last, 'How are you doing? You look great. Are things getting easier? Brett loved you so much.' And although I know their hearts were in the right place, my patience was starting to run thin, my answers were starting to get a little more direct and tad bit snippy. That's when Halee excused us so we could grab drinks, telling me she needed to run to the bathroom, and she would meet me at the bar.

"Double fisting tonight?" The voice behind me is deep, raspy, and sexy. Chills travel from the bottom of my spine all the way to the base of my neck. I turn and meet the eyes that belong to the man with the enticing fuck me voice. He is sitting two stools down, fisting a bottle of Bud Light. My eyes wander from the bottom up; he is wearing a blue suit, perfectly tailored to his broad shoulders, and a crisp white shirt that is unbuttoned just below his adams apple. His square chin is covered by day old stubble, and his hair is long, messy, and unruly. I instantly have to stop myself from reaching over and running my hands through it. Typically, I am a short hair girl; well at least that's what Brett always had. I glance up at the picture of him that is on the wall next to me. Yep, that perfect no guard fade, up to a three. It is the same haircut he had when we met in high school. I turn back to again meet the gaze of this stranger across from me. Iron City is a small town, so why do I not know who he is?

He smiles, showing off his perfectly straight, white teeth. Lord, this man could be in one of those toothpaste commercials. He nods his head down again indicating the two drinks that are on the bar in front of me. "Oh, these. Ha." Awkward laugh, real smooth, Quinn. "No, my friend just went to the bathroom. One of these is for her."

"Her? Does that mean that you aren't here with anyone?"

I look away from our intense stare down and look around the room at all the people that are here tonight. Could it be possible he doesn't know who I am? I mean, that would make sense; he doesn't look familiar to me, maybe he is new to town. Deciding not to draw him a picture of the tragedy of my life this past year I say, "Nope, just here with a friend." I hold my hand out, "Quinn."

He takes my hand in his and I feel the electricity coursing between us. What is wrong with me? I am at the foundation dinner for my dead fiance and here I am finding myself wondering what it would feel like if this man's hands touched other parts of me. "Nice to meet you, Quinn. My name is Walker." His eyes travel down my body and then back up again, all while maintaining this electrifying connection.

"Hey, is this for me?" I rip my hand out of Walker's, and move backwards a couple steps. Halee is standing between us with a smirk on her face. She looks over at me and raises her eyebrows. "Care to introduce me to your new friend?"

"Uh-h-h… yea, sure. We just met. Walker, this is my best friend Halee. Halee, this is Walker." She reaches over and shakes his hand, although their contact doesn't seem to have the same effect on her that it did on me.

"Nice to meet you Walker. Q, your parents just got here and are looking for you. Also Brett's parents just called. They didn't make their connecting flight in from Florida. It looks like they aren't going to make it in time." A flood of relief washes through me. It's not that I don't love Brett's parents, but I have done my best to avoid them since we lost him. I know it isn't fair to his family, basically losing me after they just lost him, but it's too hard. I'm a selfish bitch.

"Ok, thanks Hales." I turn back to Walker and give him a sad smile. This complete stranger made me forget all of the hurt in my life for a few short minutes, and for that I am grateful. "It was great meeting you Walker. Maybe I'll see you later."

Just then, JR, Brett's best friend who's also on the department walks up and slaps Walker on the back. "Hey ladies, I see you have met Walker. He just moved to town to fill the open position at the FD."

That's when the reality of it all hits me-Walker is here to replace Brett. And just like that, the numbness that had disappeared for a brief moment comes rushing back.

Chapter 2

Walker

Well I wanted small town. Iron City, Michigan is definitely small with a population of 7,691. Correction, 7,692, which is exactly the change I need after the year I've had. I swear my life lately could be one of those ridiculous Lifetime movies you hear about. Dad dies, dog dies, oh and don't forget about walking in on my fiancé getting nailed from behind in my bed by someone I not only considered a friend but also a fellow brother. Being part of a fire house, it becomes more like a family, especially for someone like me who has no real family left. Something about your "brother" banging out his frustrations on your fiancé, makes living together fifty percent of the time, sharing meals and going on calls together a little more awkward.

So, here I am... running away from my former life and never looking back.

Iron City Fire Department is nothing like the fire house back in Chicago, which I think is what appealed to me the most. Just walking in the door, I already feel more at home than I have in months.

"McCoy!" shouts the Chief. "I am so excited to have you here. The officers at your last house had nothing but great things to say about you." He lowers his voice so no listening ears can hear and says, "It's extremely unfortunate what happened, but I believe all things happen for a reason, and I am glad that those events led you here."

"Thanks, Chief. I am glad to be here and get a fresh start."

He slaps me on the shoulder and says, "Let's show you around and get you settled so you will be ready for your first shift tomorrow. Thanks again for making an appearance at the benefit last night. I'm sorry that we didn't have much time to talk though."

"No problem, Chief. I was glad I could be there. Brett seems like he was a great man and even better firefighter."

"He was. Losing him was tough, for everyone, but he would want us all to move forward." He brings his hand up to my shoulder as we enter the kitchen area of the fire house. "And I can say with one hundred percent certainty that you are going to be a great fit in this house and in this town."

For the next hour I met some of the guys that I didn't get a chance to last night at the benefit and, got myself familiarized with the house and the trucks. Then I ask JR about a good place to get a haircut. He gives me directions to a salon called Studio 365 and says, "One of the girls there will be able to hook you up. They give the best fades in town. Just tell them the boys from ICFD sent you."

"Thanks, guys. I will see you tomorrow." I jump on my motorcycle, put my helmet on, and take off.

✂<✂<✂<

Studio 365 is busy, really busy. Little old ladies under dryer chairs drinking coffee. A couple of older gentlemen waiting in the corner. This salon definitely has that small town feel, and I love it. It's a welcoming place, where everyone smiles when you walk in, like they genuinely care about you. When they ask how you are doing, they really want to know the answer.

While taking it all in, I notice the pint size blonde basically skipping my way is the same girl that was with Quinn last night. Obviously, the sparks I felt between me and that fiercely stunning woman were one sided. Because after JR came over, her eyes got super wide like she just saw a ghost, and she took off like someone lit a fire under her ass. I fell asleep last night thinking of her eyes.

"Hey, I remember you. Walker, right?"

"Uh yea. Was it Halee?

"It is. Nice to see you again. What can I help you with?

"The boys down at ICFD told me someone here could hook me up. I haven't had a haircut in so long, it's starting to get out of control."

Walking over to the computer she looks at the screen like she is searching for something, then turns back to me.

"Absolutely, I think that Quinn might have time right now actually…. Quinn!!!!!"

No way. All morning, I have been thinking that I needed to find a way to track her down. There's no way it is this easy.

"Why do you insist on yelling? I am literally ten feet away, Hales." Out walks the most beautiful woman I have ever seen. Her strawberry blonde hair is hanging in curls around her shoulders. She is wearing an old faded Tigers hat, a white tank top that shows enough but not too much, skinny jeans that hug her curves in all the right places, and a pair of Converse. She looked stunning last night in that black dress but seeing her like this, casual and natural looking, it does things to me. Things I haven't felt in a long time. Those eyes, those piercing green eyes, I could get lost in them. "Do you like what you see?" With one hand on her hip and looking less than impressed, she snaps me back to reality; and I wonder how long I have been staring at her.

"He stopped in for a haircut. It looks like you have time to squeeze him in," said Halee. "The guys at the firehouse sent him in."

The woman standing in front of me, who moments ago looked radiant, now pales and she rolls her eyes, "I guess." Her reply is short and makes me feel like she would almost rather cut anyone else's hair right now. She turns and starts walking towards her chair, so I glance over at Halee who mouths, 'Sorry', with a half smile and a shoulder shrug.

About halfway through my haircut and zero word exchange, I decide to try to make small talk.

"Have you lived in Iron City long?"

"Yep."

"It seems like a great town. Everyone's super friendly."

"Yep."

Well maybe everyone except her. "I am glad that I ran into you again. You ran off so quickly last night I didn't get a chance to get your number or give you mine?"

She stops what she is doing, turns and looks directly at me in the mirror, "You know, we don't have to make small talk. It is perfectly ok if I just cut your hair in silence and then you can get on with your life, and whatever that involves." Not even giving me a chance to reply, she looks away and continues what she was doing.

Wow, this can't be the same woman I met last night. She was so sweet and intoxicating when we were standing at the bar last night. If I didn't know any better I would think she is just some bitch with zero social skills.

She finishes up and cashes me out without another word besides how much I owe her. I consider making a comment about how being rude to clients can't be great for business, but I decide to stop while I'm ahead and just leave.

I throw my leg over my bike and hear someone shouting from across the parking lot. When I look up, I see her bubbly blonde friend running towards me.

"Hey, I am so sorry for what just happened in there. Obviously, she normally isn't like that."

"Hpff, what do you mean? She was a ray of fucking sunshine." I start to put my helmet on but she places her hand on my arm to stop me.

"Please give me a second to explain."

I set my helmet back on my lap and look at her. "A year ago yesterday she buried the love of her life." My face softens. Shit. Brett. I didn't put two and two together last night, and I took off shortly after she left the bar area. Halee sees that I am connecting the dots, "I tried to tell her not to work this week but she is so damn hard headed, she said she was fine. Instead she just takes out all of her anger and frustration on everyone else. And I think you were even more of a target because of what you do. And who you replaced."

Just when I thought my life was already shit. "I just came here to take a job and get away from some shit that was thrown my way back home. I had no idea when we were chatting last night that she was the fiancé to the guy that I am replacing." Shit. I was hitting on her, and she was there still mourning the guy the whole benefit was honoring.

"Don't take any of this personally. They were together since high school. I'm not sure if she will ever get past this." She pauses, blinking multiple times as if she is trying to keep the tears at bay. After a few seconds she smiles and returns to the girl I saw when I walked into the salon thirty minutes ago. "Anyways, welcome to town. I hope you will come back to Studio 365, and I am sure I will be seeing you around."

By the time I regroup enough to come up with a reply, she is skipping back towards the salon. "Thanks Halee."

I put my helmet on, start my bike, and take off. All while thinking about the beautiful girl with bright green eyes who is broken on the inside.

Just like me.

Chapter 3

Quinn

The sunlight coming through the window reminds me that I forgot to close the curtains last night. Although, after the amount I drank, I'm impressed I even made it into the bedroom. I lift my head and look around, noticing the empty bottle of vodka on the side table. At least this time it's Tito's; last time it was some cheap shit I had never even heard of. And let me tell you, the hangovers from the cheap stuff are a lot worse than with the good booze.

BANG, BANG, BANG!

Ugh, who is pounding on my door this early in the morning. I look over at my phone and see that it is eight in the morning.

Maybe if I just ignore them, then they will go away.

BANG, BANG, BANG, BANG!

Fuck!

"Open up, Quinn, I know you are in there! Your Jeep is in the driveway, answer the door!"

I get up and make my way to the door knowing that Halee isn't going to give up until I let her in. I stumble out of the room and down the hallway. Damn, I might still be a little drunk. I try to blink a few times to clear up my vision. Yep, still drunk.

This should be fun.

I open the door to let Halee in. She doesn't even look at me, just storms past in a wave of anger.

"Well good morning to you too, princess." I say sarcastically. "You could have at least brought breakfast and some coffee since you felt the need to grace me with your presence so damn early on a Sunday."

"Quinn sit down." She points to the couch. I think about fighting her on this but considering the room is still spinning, sitting down sounds like a great idea.

"Listen, I know this past year has been rough. It has been rough on a lot of us. And I knew going into this past week that it was going to be even worse with the benefit and everything, but your behavior yesterday was unacceptable."

Confused as hell, I shoot her my best 'what the fuck are you talking about' look and say, "Hales you are going to have to be more specific. Apparently making poor behavior choices is my new thing."

"Walker!" She lets out an annoyingly obnoxious laugh. "You know that gorgeous eye candy that you were basically eye fucking at the event but then he came into the salon yesterday and you treated him like he was public enemy number one. He is new in town and you couldn't have been any more of a bitch. Luckily, I caught him outside and explained the situation to him."

I shoot a glare at her, "Situation" I say with a small chuckle. Any feelings of remorse for the way I behaved yesterday disappear. "I'm glad you were able to explain my SITUATION to him. Hales, I get that you have never had a guy stick around long enough to understand what it feels like to have a soul mate, let alone what it feels like to lose one."

Her eyes go wide. Yep, I know I just hit below the belt. Halee has a great track record of dating assholes. Not that it is her fault- she's the most kind, gorgeous person I know. And not just on the outside, she truly has a heart of gold. Halee has been my person for as long as I can remember. Not only is she my best friend, but she is also my business partner. And I know better than anyone she has been picking up all the slack at the salon without complaint since I lost Brett. But, right now my defenses are up, so if she wants a fight, then I can play dirty.

"I'm going to let that one go," she says, "considering it's been a long week, and I can still smell the vodka seeping out of your pores. But it is time for you to take a good look in the mirror and figure out if this person you have become is who you want to be. I know Brett wouldn't have wanted this for you."

"HOW DO YOU KNOW WHAT BRETT WOULD HAVE WANTED!?" I scream, "Nobody knows what he would want, because he isn't here. He died. He left me, like he always said he wouldn't. And he took my heart with him."

Sympathy takes over Halee's face, and she comes over, sits down, and wraps me up in her arms. "Oh, sweetie. I know he's gone, but you aren't. You are still very much alive, and I know that he wouldn't want you living like this. Besides the salon, you don't go anywhere. You work and then you come home and drink yourself to sleep. Brett's truck is still sitting in the driveway, his shoes are still sitting by the front door, the closet is filled with his clothes. Maybe step one is donating some of his things, and thinking about selling the truck."

"His truck is the only place that still smells like him." I sob.

I know it sounds crazy but sometimes I just sit in there, close my eyes, and imagine he is driving us somewhere. That was our thing; on his days off we would go for a drive, windows down, his ball cap on, and my feet on the dash. It was one of my favorite things that made us, us. If I get rid of it, how will I ever smell him again? I know she is right, holding on like this isn't healthy. But am I really ready to let that part of him go? I don't know about that.

One thing's for sure, I know I should find Walker and apologize for the way I acted yesterday. He didn't deserve for me to take all of my anger out on him.

✂✂✂

After consuming some much needed breakfast, laying on the couch, and binge watching three episodes of Grey's Anatomy, Halee had to leave for an early Sunday dinner with her parents. So I jump in the shower, blow dry my hair, and throw on a little make up. It doesn't escape me that this is the most effort I have put into my appearance in a year, with the exception of the fundraiser the other night. I tell myself that I'm doing this for myself, but who I am kidding? The way Walkers t-shirt stretched over his chest, the tattoos that peeked out from under his sleeves, and the strength of that jawline didn't go unnoticed for one single minute. As much as I was fighting the feelings, they all came rushing back from the previous night when I was imagining running my hands through his now tame hair.

While heading in the direction of the firehouse, I suddenly realize this will be the first time I have been there since the day before the accident.

"Hey, baby, what are you doing here?" Brett rushes over when he sees me walk into the open bay door. He picks me up and spins me around, kissing me so hard I can feel it all the way to my core.

"Brett, it's been three nights since you have been home. You can't kiss me like that and

not be able to follow through." I whispered in his ear, trying to make it perfectly clear what is in store for him when he gets home tomorrow night.

He pulls me tight and I can feel the hardness growing between his legs. "Mmm... baby, I can't wait to be buried inside you."

"Hey, you two, get a room!" JR yells from across the bay, while the other guys catcall and whistle at us.

My face blushes, and I give Brett a brief kiss, whispering in his ear, "We will finish this tomorrow." I make sure my voice is extra breathy, knowing how much it turns him on. Then I walk towards the boys, giving him a minute to address the bulge in his pants.

"JR, do you really want to pick a fight with the lady that is delivering you fresh homemade cookies?" I ask with a wink.

"Double Chocolate Chip?"

"Is there really any other kind?" I hand him the box, feeling a familiar strong arm come around my waist.

JR opens the box and takes a bite out of one and exclaims, "Ohhh Ma God! Brett, if you don't hurry up and marry this girl, I will."

Brett pulls me tight and speaks in what sounds like a growl, "Back off, JR. She's mine."

I pull into the parking lot of the fire house, fighting back the tears. If I had only known that would be the last time I would see him, I would have begged him to come home. I would of said so much more than just "See you tomorrow, babe. I love you."

I force myself out of the car. I can do this. I have to do this.

Chapter 4

Quinn

I barely make it through the door before all the guys start shouting out to me. Everything is the same as the last night I was there- the trucks are parked in the same spots, the house still smells like a mix of the soap they use to clean and the scent of fire, so ingrained into their gear no matter how often they wash them. I slow my pace as I make my way to the wall with Brett's picture and a plaque that has his last call engraved into it. Next thing I know, JR throws me up over his shoulder and carries me over toward everyone else.

"Would you put me down?" I giggle, "I am perfectly capable of walking, you know."

"I know this, but I just can't believe you are here, so I am going to get you all the way inside before you try to run." He sets me down and looks at me with that typical JR smile. He was always like the brother I never had. But, when we lost Brett, I pushed him away. I make a silent promise to myself right now to make a better effort to get together with him. "You didn't happen to bring your famous cookies, did ya?"

A wave of sadness hits me all at once-some things never will never change. "Not today, but I promise I will make you a fresh batch soon. I am actually here to see if Walker has a second to talk?"

"Oh no. Not you too?" he says with a dramatic sigh.

"What do you mean, not me, too?"

"Well, this guy has barely been here a week, and he already has all the ladies in town stopping by here, trying to stake their claim on him. He says it's just because he's the new guy and it will stop soon. But, I have to say, I was the new guy once and they never lined up like this for me."

I give him a very dramatic eye roll.

"First of all, JR, you were the new guy in first grade." A small ping of jealousy shoots through me thinking about other girls throwing themselves at Walker. What is wrong with me? I have no right to feel this way. "And second, no, I'm not here to 'stake claim' on anyone. I just simply need to apologize for my behavior yesterday, I was having a shit day, and I took it all out on him."

"Well it's a damn shame that you aren't here to throw yourself at me." My breath hitches when I hear his voice. It is the same sexy rasp that drew my attention the first night we met, "Because you are someone that I wouldn't mind catching."

I turn to see Walker coming around from behind one of the fire trucks. I never thought I would be turned on by another man in duty clothes ever again but... the way those pants fit, showing off the very obvious muscles in his legs, and his shirt perfectly taut across his broad chest, leaving little to the imagination about the definition of his abs. Ugh. And why are tattoos such a turn on for me? I want to take his shirt off and explore every single detail of the tribal symbol that I'm assuming stretches up the length of his arm, around his shoulder blade and peaks out of the collar of his shirt.

When I get up to his face, I realize that I just undressed him with my eyes for the past thirty seconds, and by the cocky smirk on his face, he knows it. Those eyes though, they are such a rich brown that when he looks at you, it's as if he is reaching into your soul.

Come on Quinn, pull it together. I clear my throat and try to act like his comment annoyed me and didn't just soak my panties, "I just wanted to stop by and say that I was sorry for how I acted yesterday."

"No worries, I have a thing for woman with a little bit of attitude. But you could make up for it by meeting me for a drink Tuesday night. The guys are taking me out after our shift is over. You can buy me a beer."

Is this guy serious? Didn't Halee say she connected all the dots about me and Brett? And I'm sure the guys here might have even mentioned everything, but he still has the balls to ask me out in front of the entire firehouse. "Sorry, I'm not really looking to date. You know, dead fiancé and all." Apparently low blows are my thing today.

"Who said anything about dating? I'm just looking to have a good time and meet new people. If we just so happen to drink too much and you beg me to come home with you for an even better time, then that's just an added bonus."

I look over at JR who is as taken aback by this comment as I am, and then direct my attention back to Walker.

Oh, I could smack that smug smirk off his face! Did I really feel bad for the way I treated this asshole? The little voice in my head is screaming 'careful, Quinn, you have always had a thing for assholes.' Shit. I need to get out of here. Quickly.

"Well, as fun as this was, I have to be… anywhere else. Sorry again for taking my frustration out on you yesterday."

As I turn to walk away he yells, "You can take your frustration out on me anyway you need to, baby. See you Tuesday!"

Not a chance in hell asshole, I think to myself as I walk away without looking back.

Chapter 5

Walker

What was that? Who was that? I am not that guy, at least not anymore, and definitely not with a girl like Quinn Harris. I have heard the whispers around the firehouse about Brett; no one has come out and said anything but I hear them. Golden boy quarterback in high school, led the team to win a state championship, on the path to marry his high school sweetheart, good friend, and even better firefighter. I heard one of the guys say Brett was who you wanted by your side when you were running into a fire. And here I am, dreaming about this dead guy's fiancé at night. It's her eyes. Don't get me wrong, I'm a man so I have noticed the way her jeans fit perfectly around her tight ass and the way her v neck dips low enough to show off her perfect cleavage. But her eyes...

DING, DING , DING

Saved by the tone. Duty calls.

✂✂✂

Stubs is the local hangout in Iron City and surprisingly for a Tuesday night, it's packed.

"Go find us a table, and I'll grab us a couple beers." JR slaps my shoulder. "By the looks you're already getting from the women in here, you might be leaving with one of them sooner than you thought."

I smile at him and head to one of the high tops in the corner by the pool tables. He isn't lying, I seem to be the main attraction tonight for these women. Unfortunately, there is only one woman I'm interested in and after the way I acted on Sunday, I can almost guarantee she will not be here tonight. JR is right, I could have any of the women in here, so why am I pining for someone who is emotionally unavailable anyways?

JR walks over and sets our beers down.

I tip my glass back and chug it. "I'm going to go grab another round of beers and some shots." Maybe I can drink her out of my mind.

"Hell yeah, that's what I'm talking about!" JR shouts as I make my way across the bar.

About an hour, five beers, and more shots than I can count later, I am feeling great. You know that feeling when you aren't quite drunk yet, when you are still in control but your face starts to get a little tingly? Yeah, that's right about where I am, and losing a little bit of control is exactly what I need after the shit month I have been dealt.

A few of the guys from department showed up, so we are all playing pool and having a great time. For the most part, I just sit back and listen to the stories these boys are throwing around. A guy they call Mack goes into a story about when they were all fucking around in the bay area playing basketball and JR hit the ball with a baseball bat, sending it flying through one of the windows. They are all laughing like it just happened, while JR's face starts to get red. "Fuck off guys, that shit was not funny. You assholes took off and left me to go tell chief on my own. He was pissed, and I had to do bitch work around the firehouse for an entire month." His comment just sends the rest of us spiraling into even more laughter. I was a little nervous moving to a new department, after being at the same house my entire career, but these dudes are cool. I think this move was for the best, and I can see myself settling in here just fine.

JR's comment was spot on- these women have been throwing themselves at me since we got here. In the beginning, I was doing a better job of letting them down easy. But with the amount of alcohol I have consumed paired with the fact that, other then my hand, my dick hasn't seen much action in weeks, I am starting to welcome the attention a little more. Even if I'm not getting it from the one person that's on my mind.

I wrap my arms around the waist of a sexy little blonde in daisy duke shorts and a tank top that leaves very little to the imagination. I am showing her how to correctly hold the pool stick when I feel those intense green eyes staring at me. I look up and, sure enough, sitting up at the bar is Halee, looking like she is deep in conversation with a guy, but next to her is Quinn. She isn't showing that guy or his friend any attention; instead her focus is lasered in on me. I start to walk towards her, making the blonde I was just draped around stomp her feet in a jealous protest.

Quinn is wearing a blue dress that shows off her toned tan legs perfectly. The tightness around her tits is more revealing than anything else I have seen her in. That strawberry blonde hair is pulled up showing off her slim neck, and I can't help but want to nibble on her exposed collar bone. I don't know if it is the alcohol talking or my raging boner but suddenly I want to put my lips all over Quinn Harris.

When she notices me noticing her, Quinn turns back to the group that she is sitting next to, pretending to be fully engaged in their conversation. "Looks like you decided to come buy me that beer after all." I regret saying it the minute the words leave my mouth.

Fuck.

Chapter 6

Quinn

I kept telling myself that I was not coming out on Tuesday night; however, when Halee suggested we go grab a drink after work, I was a little too eager to accept. But, now that we are here and I have to make small talk with the guys who just walked up and asked if they could buy our first round, I am starting to regret not just going home.

Stubs isn't very big and it is crowded tonight. I don't think that Walker even noticed we are here, but why would he? He has some bimbo in shorts that barely cover the important parts, pretending not to know how to hold a pool stick. But by the look of her and the way she is practically throwing herself at him, I'm pretty sure she knows how to handle just about any stick thats placed in her hands. I slam my drink and ask the bartender for another; if I have to be here I might as well get drunk. Just as I turn around I see that Walker has seen me. He instantly leaves the desperate bimbo at the pool table and starts making his way my direction. I do my best attempt to pretend I wasn't just jealously gawking at him with his hands all over another woman's body by turning my attention back to the two guys talking to Halee. One of them is just finishing up a story about how investment banking is so interesting.I begin to roll my eyes when Walker's lust-filled voice whispers in my ear, "Looks like you decided to come buy me that beer after all."

All the hair on my bare arms and neck stand up. How does he have this much of an effect on me? It's like my body responds and craves him in ways I have never experienced, not even with Brett. It scares the hell out of me, but for some reason, I want more.

He is so close behind me, I can feel his warm breath on my neck, and I ache for him to be closer. "So I take that as a yes?" he whispers in my ear.

Slowly, I turn to him, trying to remind myself to breathe as I say, "I came here to have a good time, and from the looks of it, you have your hands full with blondie over there." Nodding my head in the direction of the girl who is now the one jealously gawking in my direction with her hands on her hips. "You should probably get back to that."

Without breaking eye contact, "Nope, everything I want is right here." His comment melts a piece of the ice wall I have built around my heart. How is it that this man who has been nothing but infuriating can flip the switch to sweet in a matter of seconds? Brett's face pops back into my head, he was the same way.

Walker glances over at the dance floor and then brings his eager eyes back to mine, "Dance with me."

The way he says it, as if what he is saying isn't a request or a question, like he is demanding me, turns me on. I stand up, hold my hand out to him, continue our intense stare down, and consent, "Lead the way."

As song after song plays, we dance and grind like no one else is on the dance floor. He comes up behind me, places his strong hand on my stomach and pulls me back into him, showing me just how turned on he is. The more I sway my hips the more his package swells, and the more I want him. It's been so long since I have wanted a man in this way. But right now, in this moment, everything feels right.

"You are so damn sexy." he exhales into my ear.

I turn around and the electricity between us is buzzing, I look up into his intense brown eyes as we slowly start to move forward. I lick my lips in anticipation of what it will feel like to have his lips on mine. But the song changes, and I am blasted back to the reality of who I am, where I am, and what I am doing by the only song that could ruin this moment... the song that Brett and I were supposed to dance to at our wedding.

I shake my head repeatedly as my eyes begin to blur. I try to hold back the tears as run away from Walker, towards the bathroom. By the time I burst through the doorway, tears rush down my face and guilt takes over my heart.

✂<✂<✂<

After passing the line of girls gathered at the sink reapplying makeup, I stumble into a bathroom stall just in time to throw up. I wait a couple of minutes to make sure its not going to happen again. Then I head to the sink and splash my face with cold water in an attempt to pull myself together.The makeup girls are gone now and I am grateful for the empty bathroom. Then Halee busts through the door.

"Quinn, what happened out there? Walker came over looking a little panicked and insisted that

I come check on you, he is so worried. What is going on? The last time I looked over at you it seemed you two were getting along just fine. I was a little concerned you were going to undress each other right in the middle of the dance floor!"

"That song, Hales. That song is… well, was, our song... my song with Brett. I feel like I was just starting to let loose and thinking maybe I can do this. I can have fun and start to move on. And then I got smacked right back to reality." I look down at my left ring finger that up until tonight, still held my perfect ring from Brett. "I think maybe this is all still too soon."

Halee smiles knowingly at me and wipes what must be my smeared mascara from my cheek. "Look, no one is saying that you have to jump headfirst into a relationship with someone. But what you were doing out there tonight was having fun, and there is absolutely nothing wrong with that. You aren't cheating on Brett because you are attracted to another man. By the way, you would be crazy not to be attracted to Walker." Leave it to my best friend to always find a way to lighten the mood. I give her a small smirk. "You are just making baby steps in the right direction. Brett wouldn't have wanted you to be alone forever."

I let out a long sigh, she is right. Brett would have wanted me to be happy. And what I have been doing this past year has not been being happy. In fact, it has been the exact opposite of being happy. I have allowed losing him to completely consume me, and Halee is right- it's time to try to move forward with my life.

"You ready to head back out there? I was really hitting it off with Scott, the guy who bought our drinks."

"Oh god, the investment banker!?" Shooting her a look of disappointment, "Seriously, Hales, that guy is a dud. You can do so much better."

Giggling she turns towards the mirror, fluffing her hair and checking her lipstick. "God no, that was his friend, who eventually left when you and Walker decided to start dry humping-"

I slap Halee in the arm, "We were not that bad!" I hesitate then ask with worry, "Oh God, were we?"

She smiles, says nothing, and starts moving us in the direction of the door, slapping me on the ass as we head back out.

Chapter 7

Walker

I have absolutely no idea what happened. One minute we are eye locked and leaning in for a kiss, and the next minute she is running towards the bathroom.

Now I'm standing outside the women's bathroom like a creeper, waiting for her and Halee to come out. The women standing next to the door are looking me up and down, licking their lips like they are the predator and I am their prey.

Unfortunately for them, I just got a taste of what happens when Quinn Harris lets her guard down, and she is all that I can think about.

Just as I start to replay everything leading up to this moment, wracking my brain, trying to figure out what the hell I did wrong, the bathroom door swings open and out they walk. Halee strolls right by me with a grin and a wink. Behind her are those emerald eyes again, only this time they are outlined by a shade of red. Crap. She has definitely been crying. But if I'm being honest, I don't think she has ever looked more beautiful.

Quinn makes her way over to me, keeping her distance and says, "Sorry about that. Want to go sit down, have a drink, and maybe I can try to explain what just happened?"

I nod and, after stopping at the bar to grab a couple drinks, we head over to an empty table. After we sit, I find myself just staring at her, while she seems lost in thought, looking deeply into her cocktail.

"Was it something I did?" I ask, worried that if I didn't break the silence, then we would sit there the rest of the night, without her looking at me.

"No…" she sighs and her sad eyes meet mine. "Not you, it was the song." I think back to that moment, trying to remember what song was playing. But I was so wrapped up in the moment with her, the anticipation of her full lips touching mine that I don't think I heard anything over the sound of my heart beating. "That was the song that was playing when Brett asked me to 'be official'. We were sitting in his truck outside my house our junior year of high school. We were both sweaty and gross from football and cheer practice. Right after he asked, that Rascal Flatts song came over the radio, and he said 'whenever I hear this song, I will remember the start of our forever.'"

Damn, I don't know what part of that confession I am held up on the most, the fact that she was a cheerleader in high school and my pervy brain is trying to imagine her in a short ass skirt, or the ping of jealousy that just hit me because she and Brett have a song. They have a past.

She looks down at her drink and continues, "Walker, I like you. Something about you draws me in and makes me want to know more. Where did come from? Are you close with your family? What made you decide to be a firefighter? Have you ever been in love? I want to know everything." She blushes, then her face turns serious and she looks at me with sad eyes. "But right now, I don't feel like I am emotionally ready to jump into another relationship. However, that doesn't mean I want you to give up on me. Unless that is unfair of me to ask. In that case, then I completely understand if you want to move on to someone who isn't damaged. Because that is exactly what I am. I haven't felt whole in just over a year, and if we are being real with each other right now, I don't know if I will ever move past losing him. And I'm sure there are at least twenty women in this bar tonight who would give you exactly what you want-"

I interrupt her, "They can't."

I let everything she just said soak in; she thinks she is broken. Maybe you can blame it on my hero complex, but I want to be the one who puts all of her pieces back together. Her eyes narrow, but before she says anything else I explain. "They can't give me what I want, because I want you, and I will give you all the time you need to wrap your head around this." Pointing between the two of us, "I'm not going anywhere, Quinn. That's a promise."

She gives me a sad smile and says, "Don't make promises you can't keep."

✂<✂<✂

During my shifts this week all I can think about is that night at the Stubs. We sat there until closing time just talking and getting to know each other better. Eventually, Halee and JR came over and joined us. They told stories about crazy things they all did in high school, with such detail it made me feel like I was there. A lot of them had to do with Brett, but, surprisingly, that didn't bother me. Instead it made me a little jealous that he got to be apart of it all with Quinn, and I didn't.

At the end of the night I walked the girls to their car, kissed Quinn on the cheek, and drove home. That was four days ago, and I have been dying to see her or hear her voice again. Luckily I was able to pick up a couple shifts, and it has been busy. So work has helped keep my mind from wandering off in her direction.

My phone vibrates springing me back to the present. It's a text message from a number I don't recognize. At first, I am a bit hesitant to open the text because my crazy ex has been blowing up my phone and social media accounts since I left.

Hey it's Quinn. Hope you don't mind but I got your number from JR. I was wondering if you have plans tomorrow. It's Sunday, so I have the day off...

I glance up from my phone and look at JR across the room. I could seriously run over there and hug that bastard right now. A big smile spreads across my face.

Me: I don't mind at all actually. I have been thinking about you. ALOT! And I would love to hang out tomorrow. What do you have in mind?

Quinn: Well this might sound crazy and if it's too much then you can totally make up an

excuse. Like you have to go to your friend's cat's wedding.

I laugh out loud… she is funny. What she doesn't know is I would do just about anything to spend time with her.

Me: Lucky for you, my friends cats wedding was last weekend. So it looks like I'm free.

Quinn: Well, I need to pack up the rest of Brett's stuff and take it to the local shelter. Halee originally told me she would help, but something came up. She suggested I ask you for help… you know, since the boxes will be heavy, and you have… big muscles...

Just then the tone goes off…

Me: Me and my muscles will be there, just send me the address and time. Gotta go. See ya tomorrow.

Chapter 8

Quinn

Walker isn't going to be here until ten thirty, so why I am up and pacing at seven? I don't understand the feelings that are racing through my body right now.

Sadness, about taking this next step with Brett's stuff and moving forward. Once his stuff isn't taking up space in the closet and dresser, the harsh reality of him really being gone will hit.

Uneasiness, is it ok to have another man in the house Brett and I shared together? Especially a man that has been the star in my not-so-innocent-wet dreams lately?

Excitement, to finally get to be spending some alone time with Walker. Even though today is going to seriously suck- I think that him being here will make it easier.

Halee thought she was being sneaky and bailing at the last minute, but I am onto her ways. Especially after she nonchalantly suggested that instead of doing it another weekend, that I ask Walker if he was available to help.

After picking up the house for the third time, showering, and blow drying my hair it's finally ten. I throw on a pair of denim shorts I know are probably a little too short and my favorite grey tank top. On my way out to the living room I light a couple candles to make it smell like sugar cookies, and then I wait.

DING DONG

I take in a deep inhale and let it out. Here goes nothing.

I open the door to find gorgeous Walker leaning against the door frame, holding two coffees and a brown bag. His hair is getting longer again and he is rocking that super sexy just-rolled-out-of-bed look.

"I called Halee to see what your choice of coffee and breakfast was; I hope your best friend knows you as well as she thinks she does." He winks.

I wave him in, shutting the door behind him. "Well, let's see... I don't drink coffee, so that will be a warm chai latte, and in the bag will be an everything bagel with plain cream cheese. How'd she do?"

"Nailed it."

"Mmmm, thank you! But you really didn't have to do that." I take a drink of my latte while I watch him set the bag down on the counter and slowly walks towards me.

He leans in close, takes a deep breath and whispers in my ear, "Ok, one rule for today. If you expect me to be a gentleman and keep my hands off of you, then you cannot make that moaning noise again."

Surprising both of us, I say with a trembling voice. "Who said I wanted you to be a gentleman?"

He pulls back. We are staring at each other, while the heat spreads through my veins. I bite down on my lower lip, he brings his thumb up and pulls it out. "Ok, two rules. You also are not aloud to bite your lip like that."

There is an emotional war going on inside my body. Part of me wants to rip his khaki cargo shorts down, pull his unfairly tight white tee off, and just take in every bit that he has to offer. But the other part snaps me out of my trance and reminds me we are leaning against the same counter that Brett used to make love to me against. I turn away, trying to get control of my breathing I say. "We should probably get to work."

"I'm following your lead today." Realizing he means that in more ways than one, I lead him back towards the bedroom where I have a dozen or so boxes ready to start packing.

I decide to tackle the dresser, and he takes on the closet, figuring it might be less awkward for me to go through Brett's underwear drawer than it would be for Walker.

"Tell me something about you. I feel like you know so much about me but I know very little about you, Walker McCoy." We met only a couple of weeks ago, but I feel like my whole life has been laid out for him, and we haven't really spoken much of his past.

He stops what he is doing, turns and leans against the wall. Running his hands through his already messy hair, he asks "What would you like to know?"

Everything.

That's the first word that comes to mind and it almost escapes my lips. Instead, I say, "Anything. Whatever you want to tell me."

"Well, let's see. I was born and raised in a small suburb outside of Chicago. I'm an only child. My mom passed away my senior year of highschool in a car accident, and I was in the car with her. A truck ran a red light and smashed into the drivers side of the car. She died on impact, and I walked away with barely a scratch. I guess seeing the way the first responders swooped in like they were real-life heroes and handled everything was what made me decide I wanted to do the same."

My mouth goes dry as my mind draws the picture he has just described. Instinctively, I want to walk over and wrap my arms around him, but instead I stay put. "Walker, I am so sorry." I wait for him to respond but he doesn't. "And your dad?"

He turns back to the closet and starts yanking shirts off hangers, "He's gone, too. Died last fall, cancer."

This time I can't fight it, I walk over to him, wrap my arms around his waist, and rest my cheek on his back. His whole body stills at the contact, "You are not alone… don't for one minute think that you are. You have me." I am not sure what made me say those words, but it's what came out, and I instantly realize, it is the truth. I may have lost Brett, but this man has lost everyone close to him.

He turns around so we are chest to chest; and I realize this is the first time I have really felt how toned he is underneath his shirt. The other night at the bar, we danced and grinded on each other but I don't think I ever let my hands wander along his hard torso.

Walker lays a light kiss to the top of my head and lets out an exhale. I wish I knew what is going through his mind right now. "Thank you, Quinn."

><><><

A few hours later, we finally tape up the last box. Walker was so sweet the entire time, making small talk when he could tell I needed it, giving me little pieces of information about him. But he also gave me space when I needed a minute to just take everything in.

He kept his hands to himself, but occasionally he would brush up against me with various body parts. Or I would "accidently" back up into him with my butt. I didn't miss the moments when I caught him ogling my chest as I was bent over. It took everything I had not to drop whatever I was holding and let him take me to the bed. Apparently it didn't occur to me when I asked him to help, that we would literally spend the entire day in my bedroom, where there's a perfectly good bed. And I'm certain that was exactly what was going through Halee's mind when she came up with this whole idea. As mad as I think I should be at this set up, I'm not; today helped me see a side of Walker that I admire. He has been through so many obstacles in his life, and he still has such a positive outlook about life. I love that.

Love.

I never thought that feeling would be possible again, but with Walker McCoy, I can feel that ice wall slowly melting away piece by piece.

"Penny for your thoughts," Walker breaks me out of my daze. We are in his truck on our way to the shelter to donate Brett's stuff. He would love this, we always said he would give the shirt off his back to someone in need. And other than a couple of my favorite hoodies, all of his shirts, pants, and shoes will go to someone who truly needs it. That puts a smile on my face.

"I'm just thinking about how much Brett would love this. Knowing that all of his things will be donated and used to help others, is exactly what he would want. Thank you so much for helping me, I don't know if I would have made it all the way through without you. Your… muscles, were a huge help" I shoot him a teasing smile and a wink.

He reaches across the truck and places his hand on top of mine, and without looking away from the road he says, "Quinn, I would do anything for you. Thank you for trusting me enough to let me into your world like you did today."

With that, we drive the rest of the way in silence, but he never lets go of my hand.

Chapter 9

Walker

After we dropped everything off at the shelter I asked Quinn if she wanted to grab dinner but she said it had been a long day emotionally and asked if she could have a rain check. Disappointment hits me but try to I understand. I can't imagine what she is feeling right now. She lost the love of her life and not the way I did. Trust me, I'm not that I'm saying Amy was the love of my life but I definitely loved her. At least I thought I did.

The afternoon I caught Amy cheating on me, I was done. I never once thought about staying and trying to work things out. I packed my bags and went to a hotel, leaving behind everything I couldn't fit in my three suitcases. Ideally, I would have gone to the firehouse but, considering she was in bed with a fellow brother, I thought the hotel was the safer bet. Going to jail for beating his face in wasn't exactly on my To Do list. So after a week in a hotel and turning in my resignation, I saw a listing for the opening here in Iron City, which led me to sitting next to this beautiful woman who thinks she is broken. And I want nothing more than to be the one who fixes her. But does she want to be fixed? Brett didn't cheat on her, in fact, from what I've heard, they were crazy in love. Soulmates, if you believe in that kind of stuff. How do I compete with someone's soulmate?

As we pull up to her house, I keep the truck running but jump out and run around to open her door.

"Thanks, but seriously you don't have to keep opening my door." She blushes.

"Yeah, I do, and I also have to walk you up to your door." What I don't say is that I am kind of hoping to steal a kiss. After that night at the bar, all I can think about is having her lips on mine again.

When we get up to her step, she gets out her keys and turns to me but avoids making eye contact. Looking down, she plays with her keys like she is trying to find the right one, but I know this tactic, she is stalling. But why?

"Quinn?"

She looks up at me through her long eyelashes and her eyes are on fire. Yeah, she wants this too.

I swallow and reach up to push her hair out of her face, "I really want to kiss you. Your lips are all I have thought about since Tuesday, but I get it if you aren't ready for this. It has been a long day and-"

She jumps into my arms and slams her lips into mine. She pulls away quickly with a look of embarrassment, but I rectify that by grabbing her hips and pulling her back to me. What was just hard and rushed is slower this time, so we can take it all in. My tongue slowly slides in between her lips asking for permission to enter her mouth, and when her lips open slightly I go all in and push her up against the wall. Our hands are everywhere on each other. She tugs at my hair, while my hands work their way down and palm her ass. I can feel myself getting hard and our bodies are so close I know she can feel it, too. I have to stop before I lose all control, burst through her door, and carry her to the bedroom. Slowly, I start to pull away and she lets out a moan, making it obvious she doesn't want this to end either.

We stand with our foreheads touching, both breathing heavy, "Babe, if we don't stop now, I don't know if I will be able to stop at all. I want you, all of you, but I also want you to be sure that you want me too. When I make love to you for the first time, I want to know that you are mine. And I definitely don't want you to regret it. But right now, I know you are still conflicted."

She is still slightly panting, trying to catch her breath, "You're right." Looking defeated, she looks down at her hands and starts playing with her keys again.

I pull her chin up with my hand and look her straight in the eyes, "Don't get me wrong. I want you, I just want all of you." Placing my hand on her heart, "That includes this, I want your heart, too, Quinn."

There it is, that smile that I have come to love in the short time I have known her. It's almost like it has become my personal goal in life to make sure she doesn't lose that smile again.

She leans up, places a kiss on my cheek, and whispers in my ear, "I don't deserve you, Walker McCoy." And with that, she unlocks her door, and walks in, only turning around to say, "See you soon."

Then she shuts the door, leaving me to stand on her front step, with a major case of blue balls.

Chapter 10

Quinn

Shutting the door was probably one of the hardest things I've had to do in a while. Minutes later I find myself still leaning against the door, holding my lips, trying to grasp what had just happened. When our lips finally touched it was like fireworks going off inside of me. My whole body felt like it was on fire, and I started feeling tingly in all the right places.

How is it possible that it never felt this way with Brett? We were together for over ten years. Don't get me wrong, our sex life was great, but what just happened with Walker, that was mind blowing, and it was only a kiss. The way he pushed me up against the wall, dominating my mouth with his and grabbing my ass had me desperate to beg for more.

Walker McCoy owns me. After what we just experienced, there isn't any going back. If he wouldn't have stopped when he did, I would have let him take me right out there on my front porch. But he is right, I am conflicted. As much as I want him, my heart breaks at the idea of moving on.

There is only one person I need to talk to right now, and that means I have to go somewhere I haven't been in over a year.

The cemetery.

✂✂✂

I have avoided coming here since the day we buried him. My mom has asked a couple times if I have come to see the headstone, since it wasn't there the day of the funeral, but I haven't had it in me.

Until today.

It is a beautiful day. The birds are chirping, and other than a couple walking their dog down by the river, I am here alone. I sit on the ground with my back against the stone.

"Brett."

I let out a long sigh. "I'm sorry this is the first time I've visited. This year has been so hard without you, and, to be honest, for the longest time I wished I died that day with you. I was so angry that you were gone. I think in a lot of ways, I am still angry. This wasn't what we had planned. You were my forever and I was yours, but you didn't hold up your end of the deal."

I turn to face his headstone, using my fingers to trace the words that are engraved on it. "You promised me this wouldn't happen. You remember? That day, we were out on JR's family's boat, and you told me you had decided not to do the college thing. Instead you were going to go through the fire academy." I blink away the tears, "I hated the idea, Brett. You knew it, too. I could tell by the way you kept reassuring me it was all going to be ok. You promised me that you would be safe and that I was stuck with you forever."

My head drops into my hands as I recall that beautiful summer day. Life was so easy for us back then. Our biggest concern was whose house the party was going to be at, and what we would tell our parents so we could stay out all night together. "There was no way you could've known what would happen at the fire that day. I know that. Or else you wouldn't have gone back in there. But running back into that house was reckless, and it broke your promise, because I don't have forever with you anymore. And God, Brett, what I wouldn't give to just have one more day."

"You'd be so disappointed in me. I've been a shitty person this past year." My eyes blur again. I swallow a few times trying to hold back my tears, but it's no use.

"I haven't been a great friend to Hales. I've snapped at her over absolutely nothing, and really she is the person who has been keeping my life afloat. I completely shut out my parents, your parents, JR, everyone, which I know isn't fair. They all lost you, too. I promise to make a better effort to let them all back in, but it's just so hard without you here." I laugh, "I always did say that I am pretty sure my family loved you more than me most days. We all miss you."

"Brett, I met someone…" I swallow the spit that has formed in my mouth and wait, as if he is going to yell at me. "That's crazy right? I mean it has only been a year. That is way too soon to move on. But, Lord help me, he reminds me so much of you. It figures that I would find someone like you, or, I guess, maybe he is the one who found me."

I laugh out loud again thinking back to the day I went to see Walker at the firehouse, "He can be a real asshole sometimes, which seems so ironic since you always said that was the reason I fell in love with you. He says things that come off so arrogant, but I can see in his eyes, just like I could yours, it's all for show. He is also a firefighter. Crazy, right? The one thing I said I would change about you. The guys down at the department seem to be accepting him as one of their own, especially JR, even though I think he is slightly jealous of all the attention Walker is getting from the women in town.

I look over near the old oak tree where a couple of squirrels are chasing each other up and down the trunk. "He kissed me today. Well maybe I kissed him first, but you probably already know this. Is it nuts that it felt so wrong but so right at the same time? Is it possible to be in love with two people? God, I am so broken, Brett. I just wish you were here; I need you to tell me what to do. He makes me smile again. And I think there is a real possibility of a future with him, but what does that mean for me and you?"

I look up and see an elderly man putting flowers on a grave. "He came over and helped me pack up all of your things to take to the homeless shelter. He asks me about you and seems genuinely interested. I think, if this was another life, then you two would have been friends."

I hear someone sniffle behind me. Quickly, I turn around and see Brett's mom standing less than three feet away with tears streaming down her face. Oh my god, did she just hear everything I just said? The tears tell me she heard at least part of it, and my heart races.

"Mrs Rhodes, I didn't hear you walk up. When did you get back from Florida?" I jump to my feet, suddenly feeling embarrassed by the conversation I just had with my dead fiancé.

She doesn't say anything; instead she walks over, wraps her arms around me, and just holds me tight. The dam inside me breaks, and I lose any shred of control that I had left. We stand there for what feels like minutes, sobbing onto each others shoulders, silently remembering the love that we both lost. When we finally pull away, she holds my face in both her hands and says, "Sweet girl, Brett loved you more than anything in this world. I remember the day he came home from school talking non-stop about this girl with strawberry hair in one of his classes. I knew that day you would be an important person in my son's life. The love you two shared is something to be admired, you two loved hard."

She pauses, giving me a second to absorb what she is saying. "But he is gone now Quinn, and he would want you to be happy. If this young man is bringing back the beautiful smile my son loved, then I think you need to see where that relationship can go. I know Brett would want this, and you have my full support... not that you need it."

There is no way to stop the steady stream of tears flowing down my cheeks. She heard everything.

"Thank you" I finally choke out. A wave of relief floods my body, as the embarrassment I was just feeling drifts away. "Knowing that you support me and this, makes me feel like Brett would, too."

We sit down, both of our backs resting against the headstone of a man we both loved with everything we had. We sat there, talking, crying, and laughing for hours. It was exactly what I needed. Being with his mom brought back a sense of closeness and peace that I have been missing since I lost him.

When we say our goodbyes I promise to keep in touch, and she surprises me by saying "I would love to meet this guy of yours someday. He must be someone really special if he has captured your heart. Love you, sweet girl."

Chapter 11

Quinn

Everything seems to change after that day at the cemetery; normal day-to-day things start getting a little easier. When I fall asleep at night, I no longer find myself soaking my pillow with tears. Instead I fall asleep while texting or talking to Walker. He has only been in my life for a little over two months, but he has quickly become the constant that keeps me grounded. Since that day we basically behaved like horny teenagers on the front step of my house, we haven't kissed. I can tell he wants to make a move, and I know I want him to, but he seems adamant to wait until I'm ready.

It just works out that I don't work on Sundays, and so far, he hasn't been scheduled to work one. So Sundays have become our thing.

He comes over with breakfast, and we binge watch Netflix while eating on the couch.

Around lunch time, we consume all of the snack food in my kitchen, while continuing whatever marathon we have chosen for the day. Then in the evenings, we give the couch a break and get up to make dinner together.

We eat dinner at the table, clean the kitchen and then plant our butts back on the couch to watch a movie. We haven't yet left the house to venture out into the world together. Instead, we stay in this little Quinn-and-Walker bubble, where we pretend that the sexual tension isn't about to boil over.

Typically throughout the day, physical touching is limited, so evenings have become my favorite. We turn all the lights off, he sits at the end of the couch with the chaise on it, and I place my head in his lap, my body laying in the opposite direction. Other than when he occasionally runs his hands through my hair, there is no contact. And it drives me insane. Sometimes, I am not even paying attention to the movie because I have my own movie playing in my head of what would happen if we would just give into the temptation.

✂✂✂

It's Saturday night, Walker is on shift, and, if I'm being completely honest, today is one of the worst days I've had in awhile. After fighting back and forth with my own emotions, I finally decide that it is time to sell Brett's truck.

I know it was time for it to happen, and I had convinced myself I was ready. In fact, I told Walker and Hales I didn't need them here today- I was going to be just fine. But I'm not ok, and do you think my stubborn ass will just call one of them to admit I need them? No. Instead, I have been in my bed listening to Rascal Flatts on repeat for two hours, once again soaking the pillow with my salty tears.

My phone on the nightstand lights up, and, for a split second I hesitate to reach for it. It's probably just Halee checking on me... again.

Walker: Hey, babe. Haven't heard from you today. Just wanted you to know I'm missing you something fierce. I know that you wanted to do this alone, but know that you don't have to be alone. I'm here.

This man.

I truly do not deserve him. He came into my life exactly when I needed him and tore down all of the icy walls I had built. Instead of being jealous or annoyed that I still have rough days, he is understanding and kind.

Me: How did I get so lucky?

Walker: Huh?? You lost me, babe.

Me: You! How did I get so lucky to find someone like you? I don't think you understand how much you have come to mean to me, Walker McCoy.

Me: I am doing ok. But today was definitely a lot harder than I expected. I should have listened to you and accepted your offer to be here for me.

Walker: Do you want me to see if I can leave? Damnit, I knew I shouldn't have covered this shift. Why don't you call Halee? You know that she will be there at the drop of a dime.

Me: Hey! I'm fine... I think I am just going to get a giant bowl of peanut butter ice cream, curl up in bed and watch some sappy chick flick.

Me: *thinking face emoji* Ohhh... maybe The Notebook. Plus, there is this guy who shows up at my house every Sunday right around eight... he seems to do a great job at making me smile. Eight is only like ten hours from now, I think I can hold out.

Walker: The Notebook huh? Is there any nudity in that one?

Me: Have you never seen The Notebook? Seriously!?!? And sorry, no nudity.

Me: Perv *wink face emoji*

Walker: I have never seen it, and if there isn't any nudity, then I'm out. No way am I sitting through a chick flick that has zero boob action.

Me: *eye roll emoji*

Our conversation continues on like this for about another thirty minutes, until I hear the dead bolt unlock and someone open and close my front door.

My heart rate increases as I walk out of the bedroom, turn the corner, and I run face first into Halee. "Jesus Hales! You could've at least called out that it was you!"

My best friend, carrying two pints of Ben & Jerry's PB&Cookies ice cream replies, "Well who else would it be? How many people do you give out house keys to?" She grabs two spoons out of the kitchen drawer, makes her way over to me; pushing my favorite dessert into my hands. "A sexy fire birdie told me you were having a bad night and needed ice cream. Also we are NOT watching *The Notebook*. That's where I draw the line." I swear she is the only female in the world who doesn't love anything Nicholas Sparks.

As we climb onto my bed, she grabs the remote and scrolls through the movie options on Netflix. When I grab my phone I find that I have a couple missed texts from Walker.

Walker: Ok ok. I will watch the movie with you. No need to give me the silent treatment.

Walker: Quinn... I already gave into your chick flick demands! You can talk to me again!

Me: Halee just got here, with ice cream... Thank you!

Walker: Anytime, babe. I wish it could be me, but since it can't I suppose Halee is the next best thing. *wink face emoji*

Walker: I will see your face shortly after eight. Sleep well, beautiful.

Me: I can't wait. Be safe if you get a call, and if you don't... dream of me.

Walker: Always.

After I set my phone down, I realize that Halee is about a third of the way into her pint and staring at me. "Why are you looking at me like that?"

"That smile. I'm glad it found its way back to your face again, Q." She turns her attention back to the TV screen and pushes play on the movie she has picked. "Oh, we are watching a zombie movie, and I am staying the night. Hope that's cool."

I lean my head over and rest it on her shoulder. "I love you, Hales."

"Love you, too."

"Oh, and Hales."

"Yeah?"

"You gotta be gone by eight."

Her body shakes slightly as she giggles. "You got it."

Chapter 12

Walker

Over the past month, Quinn and I have developed a habit of hanging out on Sundays and text a lot throughout the week. She told me about going to the cemetery and running into Brett's mom. Honestly, I think everything changed after that for us. She hasn't been as closed off towards me, and she is open to whatever this is we are doing. But other than playing house on Sundays, cuddling on the couch, our days have been pretty PG. It seems to be working for both of us though; we are really getting to know each other before jumping in.

She did sell Brett's truck, and even before she was ready to admit it outloud, I could tell it was hard on her. It killed me not being able to be there. But I was glad that, when I called Halee, she jumped right up and did what I wasn't able to do.

It's Saturday morning and, although we typically reserve Sundays for each other, I have the night off. Seeing her is the only thing on my mind.

Me: Hey, babe. How about going out to dinner tonight?

I stare at my phone for a few minutes, waiting for that little bubble to pop up. I know I'm whipped, the guys down at the station tell me on a regular basis. But there is something about her that leaves me constantly wanting more. After about ten minutes, I realize she is probably busy at work, so I put my phone down and start my work out.

While jogging on the treadmill in my home gym, insecure thoughts go through my head... maybe she isn't busy at work? Or maybe I'm just her Sunday person and she doesn't want to give me another day? God, I'm seriously losing it. Pull your shit together, Walker, she is just a woman.

But I know it isn't true; she isn't just a woman, she is the woman. The one I am starting to imagine a life with, something I never thought I would do again after Amy. Is it possible to fall in love with someone in just six short weeks?

The music in my headphones cut off, and my phone pings from across the room, letting me know I have a text. I practically fall off of the machine trying to get to it quickly in case it's her.

Quinn: Hey! Sorry, work is so crazy busy that I am just now checking my phone. I would love dinner, but why don't you come over, and I will cook. We can stay in and watch a movie or something.

Or something? I can think of about a million somethings I want to do to her body. Just the idea of her in the kitchen cooking dinner for me makes me want to go all caveman and claim her as mine.

Me: Are you sure you are up for cooking? I can just pick something up on the way over, too, if you are too tired?

Quinn: Totally fine... maybe I can recruit you and your "Muscles" to help. *wink face emoji*

Me: Sounds good. Your place around 5? I will bring the wine?

Quinn: Perfect! Can't wait to see you.

Me: Same

✀<✀<✀<

On my way over to Quinns, I stop at the store to grab her favorite bottle of white wine. It's one of the many things we have talked about over the past few weeks. I think tonight is the night; I have to tell her how I am feeling. Yeah, we have been hanging out a lot which leads to the occasional snuggle, but still I feel as if we are in the friend zone... I want out. I need to know exactly where her head is at, and if she is thinking that this could be long term, like I am.

Quinn is standing in the front door as I start to walk up the steps, looking sexy as hell in her black leggings and low cut tank top. It's one of the many things that attracts me to her, she doesn't over do it. Yes, when she is at work she is done up and don't get me wrong, it does things to me to see her like that.

The last time she cut my hair, she kept "accidentally" pressing her boobs against different parts of my body. At first it was just a light graze on my arm, then she leaned forward to "adjust my cape", and her perfect tits bumped into my neck or the back of my head. But the worst, or maybe best, time was when she was leaning in front of me to trim up my facial hair. Her v neck top did nothing to hide what genetics blessed her with, and made one specific part of me grow painfully hard.

But the way she is dressed right now, with her hair piled on top of her head, exposing her neck like it is begging to be kissed, this is what I have grown to love. This is the Quinn I want to come home to after every shift and have her waiting in the doorway with that smile. If I didn't know better than I would think it's a fuck me smile.

She greets me with a kiss, which is completely unexpected. I welcome it and am quick to return it, backing her up into the wall of her entryway and shutting the door. Her little moans are going to be the death of me. If this is how she sounds when we kiss, then I can only imagine the sounds she will make when my head is between her legs or I'm inside her.

"Hi." she says, out of breath when we finally pull away. Part of me wants to ask what has changed, but the other part of me doesn't want to question it and risk her shutting back down.

"Hey."

"I already have the chicken in the oven, I just need to peel the potatoes and get them boiling. Comfort food sounded good. Hope that's ok?"

"That sounds great, but I can think of some other things I would like to peel off… starting with this tank top." I slowly lift the hem of her shirt.

She blushes and slaps my arm, "Hey mister, you are supposed to be here to help cook. I can't have you distracting me. For now you better stick to peeling the potatoes. Maybe later you can help me with my clothes." She winks, grabs the wine out of my hand, and walks towards the kitchen.

I don't think she understands what she does to me. Being near her gives me a perpetual hard on, and, when she says things like that, it makes me about lose it in my jeans, right here in the hallway.

After discretely adjusting my crotch, I make my way to the kitchen to find her pouring both of us a glass of wine. For the next hour, we talk, laugh, and cook. Occasionally, one of us touches the other inappropriately, but we both just smile and continue preparing the meal. The sexual tension between us is at an all time high. I can tell we both want this. But, before it happens, I need to know where her head is at. Quinn isn't just some quick lay for me. If we take this next step then I want it to be because we are both invested in a possible future.

When we finish eating, we clear the table and head into the kitchen to do dishes. This seems so normal, like we have been doing this together our whole lives. I have never found myself wanting to be so domestic in my life. But right now, right here, with this woman… I want it all.

She is deep in thought, staring at the dishes sitting in the sink. I walk up behind her, wrap my arms around her waist and start lightly kissing behind her ear, making my way down to her collar bone.

"Mmmmm… Walker…" she moans.

Before I even know what I'm saying, it spills out, "Quinn, I think I'm falling in love with you, or maybe I am already in love with you. Hell, I don't know. But I do know that this, right here, feels one hundred percent right."

Her whole body freezes, and I can feel her heart beating like it is going to come out of her chest. What did I just do? Did I just ruin whatever we had going on because I'm a pussy who can't keep his feelings to himself? Shit.

Chapter 13

Quinn

"Quinn, I think I'm falling in love with you, or maybe I am already in love with you. Hell I don't know. But I do know that this, right here, feels one hundred percent right."

What? My whole body freezes. What did he just say? He loves me? I should say something, right? But what?

I have only ever told one man I loved him. One man I thought I would love for the rest of my life. But Brett isn't here; Walker is. He just confessed his love to me, and I'm standing here like a fool trying to come up with the right words to say back.

Do I love him? I don't have the answer to that. I think I definitely could love him eventually, but could I possibly be there yet? Come on, Quinn, say something. Anything.

"Thank you…" Crap. Anything but that.

I turn to look him in the eyes. "Walker, I didn't mean to say thank you. To be honest, I don't really know what to say."

He brings his hand up and cups the side of my face, looking deep into my eyes. "Babe, you don't have to say it back. I know you might not be there yet, but I have been feeling this way for awhile. I felt like I was going to explode if I didn't say something. I'm confident in us, and even if you aren't fully there now, I know you will be eventually. And that is enough for me, I am willing to wait."

All of the air is stripped out of my body, I lunge into his arms, our mouths meet, and it's as if this is the last time we will ever get to kiss one another. His arms wrap around my waist as he lifts me up onto the counter, my hands touching every part of him I can reach. I pull at the hem of his shirt, and in one swift motion he reaches behind his neck and yanks it off, discarding it somewhere on the floor.

Good God, he is perfect.

"Oh, you like what you see, babe?" He says with a smirk.

Shit, did I just say that out loud?

I run my fingers along his chest, paying attention to every little divet between his abs, making my way down to the perfect V that begs for my attention. It should be illegal to look this way. Instantly, my mind betrays me as images of Brett take over, and I start to compare the two men.

I knew Brett when he was a young, scrawny bean pole. With age, he filled out because of sports and then grew into his man body. But what I am looking at now, he never had all this. Guilt starts to overwhelm me, but I decide to push it away.

Why am I fighting this?

I want this. I want everything Walker and I have started to build together. And in order to move forward with him, I have to accept that Brett is in the past. Obviously, I will never forget him, but to be fair to both Walker and myself, I have to try to move forward. I can't think of a better man to help me do exactly that.

"Quinn, talk to me. Is this ok? I don't want to do anything unless you are completely sure. As much as it will kill me, I can put my shirt back on.

We can go out to the living room and watch a movie like we planned."

"No! For the love of all things holy, do not put that shirt back on!" My hands are still tracing each abdominal ripple. "In fact, new rule, you can never wear a shirt, like ever again. It should be against the law to hide this." His smile creeps back, giving me the cocky grin that seems to consume my thoughts.

"Walker," I pause, overthinking exactly what I want to say to him at this moment. I would never want him to think I reciprocated these feelings just because he said them. "I think I'm falling for you, too."

His eyes widen, he clearly wasn't expecting those words to come out of my mouth right now. Before he can say anything, I continue. "I didn't know if that would ever be possible again, but I find myself imagining what our life could look like. I want this. I want you, all of you." While my confession sinks in, my hands slowly make their way down his sculpted torso, and this time I don't stop. His eyes widen even more as I start to undo the button of his jeans.

"Did you hear me, babe? I want all of you. Now" I whisper.

Our mouths, like magnets, only part when it is required to take off our clothes. Once he removes my bra, his mouth quickly finds my breasts. While his lips tends to one, his fingers are kneading the other. I strongly inhale and exhale slowly. " Don't stop. Please don't stop."

Reaching between his legs I find his already hard shaft throbbing, begging for some attention. I stroke him slowly, and he lets out a long, agonizing moan, leaning his face into my neck. "Quinn, babe, you can't do that. My dick has wanted this since the minute I first saw you. If you keep touching me like this,I'm going to blow right here."

"Take me to the bedroom, Walker."

Before I can even get all the words out, he lifts me off the counter, both hands gripping tightly on my ass. I wrap my legs around his sturdy waist as he makes his way to my room, our mouths never leave each other. When we reach the bed, he gently lays me down and looks at me with such lust, every part of my body tingles in anticipation.

He leans forward, runs his fingers along the inside of my panties and up my slit, "Fuck, Quinn. You are so wet for me. I have to taste you." His hands rip my underwear off in one swift motion and his mouth is on me. He licks and sucks my clit with an intensity that drives me completely wild. I can't keep from moaning in pleasure.

His fingers gently slide inside me and curl up just right, finding my spot. I feel the pressure building throughout my body. God, how long has it been since I have had a orgasm? I am a bomb about to explode and I want more. "I am so close, Walker, don't stop. Please don't stop." He continues assaulting my sensitive bud until my whole body shakes, giving him everything I have.

As I come down from my orgasm, he sits up, smiles that perfect smile, and wipes his mouth with his arm. "You are amazing." he whispers. I return his smile, but quickly look away from his intense stare. How is it possible for this man's words to embarrass me when his mouth was between my legs just moments ago.

I notice him palming his erection, and I pull him down on top of me, "Hey, didn't I say that I wanted all of you? That includes this guy too." I grind my hips into his, feeling just how hard he is underneath his briefs.

"We don't have to do this, Quinn. In fact, we shouldn't do this because I don't have a condom. I didn't plan on this happening tonight. Honestly, seeing you get off like that and the way you screamed right as you hit your peak, was more than enough for me." He kisses my nose, and starts to sit up.

Once again, I pull him onto me. "No I don't think you understand. I need you. I have been on the pill since we started hanging out, so we are good there. And I am clean, so as long as you are, too." He nods to say yes. "Then you better get your impressively sized friend inside of me before I resort to begging."

Instantly, he drops his underwear, parts my legs, and slides inside of me. Once he is all the way in he stops and lets out a deep breath, "Are you ok?" When I give him a reassuring nod, he continues his slow and cautious thrusts. "Shit, you are so tight."

"Walker!"

"Yeah, babe?"

"Fuck me."

And he does. In fact, he continues to give me the most earth shattering orgasms, for the rest of the night.

Chapter 14

Quinn

I wake up to the sound of someone lightly snoring next to me. Flashbacks of last night hit me like a strobe light: the different positions, all the sensations and Walker worshiping every inch of me in ways I didn't even know were possible.

I roll over and find him still sleeping. The sheet covers only the bottom half of his naked body, leaving the top completely exposed for me to graze upon.

You would have to be crazy not to appreciate the beautiful masterpiece laying next to me. I wasn't kidding last night when I told him he should never wear a shirt again. His chiseled abs are god-like, which I know because I personally kissed and licked every single one of them.

His face though, is a whole other story. He looks so peaceful with his day-old stubble starting to show along his defined jaw, perfect kissable and talented lips and sexy bed head.

"Hey, you. Do you like what you see?" He quotes what I said to him the second time we met but without the bitterness and anger. Ugh. I was such a bitch to him. How did I get so lucky to have this man laying next to me right now.

"Hey yourself. I very much like what I see. In fact, waking up to this view everyday could make me a morning person for sure." Oh shit, I didn't mean for that to come out that way. He probably thinks I'm this crazy clinger that he slept with one time and now wants him to move in.

Panically, I try to come up with some way to retract what I just said, but he pulls me in close and softly kisses the tip of my nose, "Yeah, I have to agree. This isn't a terrible way to wake up, except maybe for the fact I am sporting a serious boner. I'm not even sure how that is possible after last night."

"Mmmmmm, last night. I have an idea to solve this issue. Why don't we continue last night's events, but in the shower? Halee is coming over today for a girls day and to talk about a new stylist she wants to hire at the salon."

He reaches under the sheet and pulls at my nipples, while moving the other hand lower towards my apex. "You mean I have to share you today?" Slowly, he slides two fingers inside of me while trailing light kisses along my neck.

I give him a pouty look and nod, as he continues to rub all the right places, kicking myself inside for making these plans yesterday with Hales. I consider all the things this man could do with my body if he was given an entire day to do them, this causes an instant pool of moisture between my legs.

"Good Lord, woman, are you ever not wet?"

"Not when you're around, have you seen yourself? You are like my own person walking porno." Just then a wave a fear hits me, what if he isn't just MY walking porno? The thought of sharing him with someone instantly makes me sick. "Wait, you are MINE right? I mean I don't want to come off crazy but I don't really share well, you know, only child and all."

He lets out that sexy laugh and brings his head to mine so our foreheads are touching. "Yes, Quinn, I am YOURS. Today, tomorrow and everyday after that, for as long as you want me. I'm pretty sure I was yours from the moment I met you.

Or it might of been the haircut that you gave me because we both know it wasn't our deep conversation that drew me in that day."

I teasingly slap him in the stomach, and he lets out a dramatic grunt like I hurt him.

"Ha, funny! You are definitely a jokester! I am so sorry for treating you that way, but there you were, standing in front of me looking like a dream. And I was still too busy starring in my own personal nightmare." So many things have changed since that day. "You helped pull me out and to truly start living again,and I will forever be grateful for that. I can't imagine a life of not knowing you, so thank you for being here with me."

He closes his eyes and takes a deep breath, what I wouldn't give to be inside his mind right now. "Hey, Walker."

"Yeah babe?"

"Will you do something for me?"

"Anything."

"Fuck me in the shower before Halee gets here?"

Within seconds, he carries my naked, eager body to the bathroom. Following through with my request. Twice.

✂✂✂

"Ugh, I hate that I told Halee we could hang out today. What was I thinking?"

He picks up his duffle bag, emptier than when he got here yesterday, and throws it over his shoulders. I suggested it might be a good plan to keep a few things here, just in case he ever forgets something. The idea of sleeping in his ICFD t-shirt and boxers has me ready to call it a day and go to bed. I am pretty sure he was onto me but he said I had a good point, pulling a toothbrush and a few other things back out of his bag. Instantly, I know that this should probably scare the shit out of me. It was just a month ago that I moved all of Brett's stuff out of here. But for some reason, I am overwhelmed with peace just knowing something of his is here. Even when he isn't.

He walks over and kisses me on top of the head, snapping me out of my thoughts. "You were thinking that you needed a girls day to gossip about all the hot sex we had last night and this morning."

Blushing, I slap him on the arm. "I will neither confirm nor deny that theory." Then it hits me, maybe he doesn't want people to know about us and what we do behind closed doors. I mean, it's just Halee, it's not like she is going to make an announcement at Stubs or anything. She always knew everything about Brett and I, from our first kiss, to when we took each others virginity, everything. But Walker isn't Brett, "If you don't want me to talk to her about us, that's ok too. I can just tell her nothing happened."

I know that as soon as my best friend sees me, she is going to know exactly what happened. In fact, she knows me so well there is a possibility that she will be able to tell how many times I climaxed. She claims it's gift, but I think it's creepy and sometimes intrusive.

He laughs, and gently grabs the back of my neck pulling me up to him. "Babe, you can tell the world. As far as I'm concerned, the more people who know you are mine, the better." He brings his lips down to mine, slowly pushing his tongue into my mouth and I give in completely. Dropping his duffle, he moves me back towards the wall, never breaking contact.

DING DONG

"She literally has the worst timing, I swear."

He laughs, backs away from me, and picks his bag back up. "It's ok, I should get going anyways."

The door opens and Halee yells, "Put your clothes on, I'm coming in." She walks around the corner, and it must be obvious she interrupted something, because she stops dead in her tracks and says, "Oh shit, I was kidding, but I can come back."

Just then, Walker's phone pings, and he pulls it out of his pocket. I can't tell who it is from where I am standing, but his whole body shifts, and his face turns white.

"Everything ok?" I ask as I move towards him.

He quickly shoves his phone back into his pocket, kisses me on the forehead, and replies, "I'll call you later. Ok? See ya, Halee." Then he walks out the door.

"Well that was weird. What just happened? I walked in here and you two looked like a couple of dogs in heat but the next second he's basically running out the door." I can tell that she is staring at me, but I'm still looking at the door. What just happened? Who was that on the phone?

"I'm sure he's fine. He has a lot of errands to run today and said he didn't want to interrupt our gossip." She smiles her megawatt smile I love and heads into the kitchen.

"Perfect, because I want every single detail of what happened last night, and it could have gotten a little awkward if he was sitting here when you give them to me." She winks. Yes, this is my best friend, always ready for the dirt; especially when it comes to my sex life. "Ok, let me guess…" She places her finger on her lips and looks up as if she is deep in thought. "I'm guessing your lucky ass got off four times last night. Am I close?"

Four? That's funny. I had four orgasms within the first hour. "You get the snacks and wine, I am going to run to the bathroom quick. I'll be right back."

"Hurry up, bitch." she hollers as I walk back into my bedroom. I make my way to the night stand and grab my phone. I just need to send him a quick text to make sure he is ok. Something or someone obviously upset him. Whatever it was, it sucked the life right out of his perfect face.

Me: Hey, you. Is everything ok?

I set my phone down and walk into the bathroom, just as Halee yells something from the living room. I couldn't make out what she said but I assume it falls under the category of "hurrying my ass up." As I'm washing my hands I hear my phone vibrate in the other room.

Walker: I'm good, babe. Just got to the station, I am going to work out here with JR then probably head home for the night. I will call you before I go to bed. Have fun with Halee.

I read his text and then set my phone down. I don't really feel like it's my place yet to pry, so I let it go. If this is something he wants to talk to me about, then he will. Quickly, I send him a reply letting him know that I miss him already. I decide to drop the subject, hoping he will feel comfortable enough to come to me if he needs to talk about something.

When I get back into the living room, Halee is flipping through my DVR. She turns and looks at me. "Jesus, I thought I was going to have to send in a rescue team to pull you out."

"Sorry, I sent Walker a text to make sure everything was ok."

"Annnnd…?"

"He said he's fine." I shrug. "So, I guess everything is fine."

"Cool, now tell me. Who's better in the sack, Brett or Walker?"

I roll my eyes, "Seriously, Hales?"

She pops up and shoves her feet under her butt getting comfortable, like it's story time. "Oh, I am one hundred percent serious right now. Up until last night you had only had sex with one man-"

I cut her off, "What makes you so sure Walker and I had sex last night?"

"Ummm.. because I'm your best friend, and your whole body screams that you had amazing, raunchy, sex last night. So, excuse me, but I want all the deets. So spill, how big is he?"

I blush and give into her questions. There is no way she is going to give up until she gets some answers. "Big enough that I was pretty sure he was going to split me in half when he first put it in."

She squeals. "I knew it! Tell me everything, you dirty slut."

We spend the next four hours eating, drinking and talking about everything under the moon. You would think that we hadn't seen each other in years, but it had only been hours. She caught me up on things with her and Scott, the guy she met that night at Stubs. I make a mental note of his name, remembering my best friend failure to come up with the last guy's name. Halee seems to be super excited about him. I should probably suggest a double date sometime soon so I can check him out for myself. My best friend is great at so many things, but picking men is not one of them.

"So tell me about this new stylist you want to bring on. Is she from Iron City, do I know her?"

Halee tells me about Charlie, a twenty-three year old girl who just moved here looking for a fresh start. What is it about Iron City that draws people in who are looking to start over? Whatever it is brought Walker here, for which I am grateful.

"Hales, I trust your judgment. If you think she will be a good fit with us, then I am cool with it. When can she start?"

She does a little jump, "I was hoping you would say that because I told her she can start this week." Halee gives me a smile that she knows I won't stay mad at. "This is going to be a great thing Q, we always said that after we were open for a year we would hire someone new. With everything that happened with Brett last year, I haven't felt like there was a great time to bring someone else on at work. But you seem to be happy and living again,

that alone makes me what to find Walker and lay a
giant kiss on him"

"You keep your lips to yourself, got it?" I
point my finger in her direction.

Halee throws her hands up in the air, "He's
all yours! I'm not really into threesomes anyways.
Well besides that one time." She winks.

Chapter 15

Walker

I glance down at my phone and once again, hit decline. Ten is the number of text messages I have received from Amy since Sunday morning, not to mention the countless phone calls and voicemails.

I don't even know what the voicemails say; I just delete them over and over again. I'm sure it's more of the same shit she is texting me. "Please call me", "We need to talk about things", "I miss you, we can work this out." What she doesn't understand is that even if Quinn wasn't in the picture, I still wouldn't go back to Amy. I put up with a lot of bullshit when it came to my ex, but cheating is one thing I will not tolerate.

What I don't understand is why she is calling now. It's like she has this radar installed in her that lets her know I am happy and moving on. So, of course she has to try to stomp all over it.

Three is the number of years I wasted on Amy. I don't think we were ever really good for each other. I just think we had the same friends and ran in the same social circle, so it was convenient to stay together. Yeah, the sex was ok, but nothing like what happened between Quinn and I last weekend. With Quinn it was mind blowing sex. The kind that keeps you up at night thinking about it until you can have it again.

I've been working a three day shift, so I thought I would stop in to surprise my girl, maybe even get a haircut. Quinn she says she likes my hair shaggy, but it's way too damn hot right now. Maybe, if I catch her off guard, she'll give me one.

As I walk into the salon, there is a new face I don't recognize sitting behind the desk. She's a petite little blonde with glasses. This woman is cute, and I'm sure she turns on most men, but she's got nothing on my girl. When she looks up from the tablet she is reading her eyes light up.

I know that look; I have been getting it from women since I was seventeen. That was the year that my acne cleared, and I bulked up from really hitting the weight room. I shoot her a polite smile, but before I can ask if Quinn is here, she nervously speaks.

"H….Hi, can I help you? Do you need a haircut? I have time right now. I could definitely fit you in." She gives me a shy smile, looking me up and down and taking me all in. I let out a laugh, thinking to myself she better hope Quinn doesn't see her ogling me with her eyes, or else she might not have a job for long.

"Naw, that's ok. Thanks. I'm actually here to see Quinn. Is she around?"

Her face drops along with her shoulders. "Oh, yeah, she's in the back room. You can head back there." She says pointing to the back of the salon.

"Thanks…Ummm..." I wait for her to tell me her name.

"Charlotte, but most people call me Charlie."

"Cool. Well, Charlie, I'm Walker. I'm Quinn's…." Well fuck, what am I? We haven't really given this a title yet. I mean, we are certainly more than friends but I don't really feel like the term "fuck buddy" is accurate either. I will definitely have to bring this up next time we are alone.

"Hell yes, you are!" Quinn walks out of the back room, and stalks towards me. Damn, it's been three days since I've seen her. We did try out some hot sexting last night but it just doesn't compare to seeing this girl face to face. My body reacts immediately when she wraps her arms around my neck, bringing her lips to mine.

"Hell yes, I'm what?"

"Mine. You said "I'm Quinns." Can we just plaster that on your back for everyone in the world to know?" She leans closer to my ear, "You think I didn't see the way she was looking at you? Can't say I blame her, I know what's going on under this uniform." She lays another kiss on me, almost like she is marking me as hers.

As Quinn leads me towards her chair she says over her shoulder, "I suppose you are going to try to convince me to cut that gorgeous head of hair?"

I am mesmerized by the way her ass moves when she walks ahead of me. So she catches me staring at it when she turns around. Busted. "Come on, babe. It's so hot out. Can we try this whole longer hair thing this winter, when I'm not sweating my balls off?"

Halee comes around the corner, "We would hate for him to lose his balls. Wouldn't we, Quinn? Hey Walker."

"Hey, Halee. See? She gets it." Pointing my thumb in the direction of her spit-fire best friend.

Quinn rolls her eyes and leans in closer, rubbing her tits all over my back. "Fine, but I'm only doing this because I've grown quite fond of your balls." She kisses me on the cheek, picks up her clippers, and starts cutting my hair.

"So, I had to put a passcode on my phone last night. I was pretty sure JR was waiting for me to set it down so he could read what we were texting. Every time I looked up he was hovering over my shoulder, trying to see what was going on." Her cheeks pink. "I have to say, for someone who has never sexted, you nailed it, babe,"

She stops mid swipe and gives me a challenging look in the mirror, "Who said I have never sexted before?"

My stomach drops. Of course she has sexted before, she was with another man for damn near half of her life. "Oh, I just thought that's what you meant when you said you had never done this before."

After a long pause, she smiles coyly and continues with my haircut. "I'm just kidding, you were my first." I pull her around the chair so we are nose-to-nose, "Good, I will take all the firsts I can get with you."

"Ok, you two, finish up that haircut and go get a room or something. You are giving out false advertising to the other customers about what's included in a haircut." Halee looks at an older man, probably in his seventies. "Don't get any ideas, Bob."

Quinn lets out that giggle I love and finishes my haircut. What I wouldn't give to hear that sound everyday for the rest of my life.

I'm hugging Quinn and saying goodbye outside when my phone goes off in my pocket. I'm sure it's Amy again. I know I should mention to Quinn that my ex has been messaging me but, I'm hoping if I just continue to ignore her, then she will give up and move onto the next guy. "Do you want to get that?" she asks, looking down at my pocket.

"No, I would much rather make out with you. I'm sure it's nothing." So that's what we do- make out like horny high schoolers under the bleachers. Only we are grown ass adults standing in front of the business she owns.

Too quickly, it's time for her to head back inside, so we exchange goodbyes. I turn back when I remember something that I was supposed to talk to her about.

"Oh, hey! JR's birthday is Saturday, I think he wants to have people come to Stubs for drinks. Are you good with that?"

"Sounds great, babe. I will see you Friday night after your shift is over? Make sure you save your stamina… you are going to need it."

"Yes, ma'am. My body is yours for the entire weekend."

Chapter 16

Quinn

It's finally Friday! I only have two more haircuts to get through, and then I am free for the rest of the weekend. I took Saturday off because Walker isn't on shift, and I wanted to spend the entire day with him.

An entire day of uninterrupted, hot, kinky, all-over-the-house-sex with this man. My client clears her throat, "I'm sorry Sally. What did you say? My mind was somewhere else for a moment." I admit with a grin on my face.

"That's ok, sweetie. Does your wandering mind have anything to do with a very handsome piece of arm candy the whole town seems to be talking about?"

Confused, I ask, "Sally, have you been talking to my grandmother again?" She gives me a mischievous grin that says it all; these old woman don't fool me. I swear, the minute my grandma found out I was spending time with Walker, she probably called every single one of her bingo friends to share the news.

"I will just say that I definitely approve, and I like seeing a smile on your face again. We all loved Brett, and losing him was hard, I know this. But you are a young, beautiful woman who deserves happiness. I'm glad you've found it again."

I give her a weak smile and, for the first time, I confess aloud the uneasiness I have been feeling inside. "You don't think this is too soon? I mean, it's been just over a year since I lost him. Am I jumping into things too fast? Do I need to take more time to grieve?"

She uses her feet to turn the chair so we are facing each other, "Now you listen to me, as long as you are happy, nothing is too soon. You can't put a time frame on things when it comes to matters of the heart. Maybe this beautiful man was sent to you because someone up there knew you needed him. I know for a fact that our sweet Brett wouldn't have wanted you to be alone for the rest of your life. Embrace this sweetie, let this man in." She turns back around and fans herself. "Lord knows, if I was just a few years younger, I wouldn't mind letting him in myself."

"Sally!" I gasp. She just shrugs in reply, and we both giggle.

Even though I've been questioning it, she is right. I deserve this, Walker deserves this and most importantly, Brett would want this for me. With every giggle I feel the shreds of doubt break away from my heart.

✄✄✄

Walker stopped by the salon today and grabbed the key to the house, stating he wanted to do something special for me. So, when I pull up and see his truck sitting there, it doesn't surprise me. Even more, it doesn't look or feel out of place; it feels right. I could get used to coming home to him everyday.

As I make my way through the door, I am caught by the smells wafting through the air- italian. He is definitely cooking something italian, but there's also a faint scent of sugar cookies. When I get to the kitchen, I find him standing in front of the stove, wearing my apron with no shirt under it.

I watch the way that his back muscles flex and his ass shakes a little as he stirs. Who knew that cooking could be so damn sexy? He looks over his shoulder and gives me that panty-dropping smile he has mastered so well.

"Are you cooking for me, Mr. McCoy?"

"I am. I hope you like spaghetti, because it's basically the only thing I know how to make."

I make my way over to him, rubbing my hands along his arms, across his back, landing on his neck, "I love pasta. White sauce, red sauce, I'm not too picky. Pasta is the way to my heart. That and you being shirtless."

He leans in giving me a kiss, "Good. Owning your heart is pretty much my end game here." Smacking me on the ass, he continues, "Go clean up. Dinner will be ready in about ten minutes."

"Yes, sir." I make my way towards the bedroom, but turn around to ask. "Do I smell sugar cookies?"

He lets out a loud laugh, "Yeah, but it's just the candle. I wasn't kidding when I said spaghetti was the only thing I can make. I did, however, bring ice cream. I thought maybe we could have some fun with it after dinner." He lifts his eyebrows at me, "Now go change, so we can hurry up and eat, before moving on to dessert."

The next hour is full of laughing, telling stories about our week and eye fucking each other from across the table. We clean up the table together, even though I tried to convince him that he cooked so I should clean. But Walker wasn't having any of that. He said "The quicker we get this done, the quicker I get you over to that couch." I have never cleaned the kitchen so fast in my life.

Even if all we did was lay entwined together and watch a movie, it would be enough for me. Being in his arms has quickly become my happy place, and I'm still not sure if that makes my heart swell with joy or scares the crap out of me. After Brett died, I told myself I would never let another person be the reason for my happiness, because if they are gone, what do I have to live for?

But here I am, diving in head first and hoping he will be there with me when I land, and more importantly, that he never leaves.

"I'm in this." I quietly say as we sit down on the couch. He wraps his strong arms around me pulling me into his lap and against his hard chest.

"What was that, babe? You good with another horror movie tonight or are you wanting to change it up?"

I clear my throat and turn so we are looking at each other, "I said I'm in this. Me and you. Coming home today and having you already here, it made me happier than I ever could have imagined. When we met, I had walls built up so high, and I had told myself I wasn't going to let anyone back in. But you were consistent, you chipped away at those walls, and now they are gone."

I look down, trying to gain the courage to say this next part. He gently grabs my chin and pulls my gaze back up to meet his. "I guess what I am saying is that I love you, Walker McCoy, and I don't want a life without you in it. I know you signed a six month contract on your house but when it expires, I want you here with me. I want to fall asleep in your arms and wake up to you snoring every morning. What do you say? Move in here?"

Who knew that this man's cheeks could pink up the way that they are in this moment? "I do not snore." he says defiantly.

"Seriously? I just confess my love for you and ask you to move in with me, and you snoring is what you comment on?" Just as the last word leaves my lips, he dominates my mouth with his, pulling me from the couch so I am now straddling his lap. I can feel him growing hard beneath me as I start to grind on him.

He pauses, and softly grabs my head with both hands, bringing our foreheads together, "Quinn, I think I have loved you since the first time I laid eyes on you in that black dress, that showed off your sexy ass collarbone." He pulls the oversized sweater off my shoulder, planting light kisses. "Or the second time when you were wearing your worn Tigers hat, those tight ass jeans and your Converse. Babe, you own my heart. Every. Damn. Piece. Of. It." He peppers me with more kisses in between those last words.

Slowly, I climb off of Walker and make my way down to kneel before him on the floor. "Woman, what are you doing? Get your ass back up here."

I shake my head in protest, undo his belt, and unbutton his pants. He lifts his hips slightly as I pull them off, discarding them beside the couch, "Nope, I want you in my mouth."

He draws a deep breath in, and then exhales as I take his stiff member in my hand. Gripping it at the base while running my tongue along the vein underneath, I make my way up to the crown. I lick the salty bead of pre cum waiting for me when I reach the top. Then, take all of him into my mouth.

"Shit, Quinn, you have me so close already." I continue stroking him, taking him deep inside my throat until he is bottoming out. I am greatly appreciative for my lack of gag reflexes in this moment because this man is huge. "Babe, you have to stop. I want to be buried deep in your sweet spot when I blow."

He pulls me up off the floor, and lays me down gently on my back, as if he would break me if he wasn't careful. "Walker, I want you inside me."

"Oh no, babe. It's my turn." He lowers himself, parting my legs and kissing every part of me as he makes his way down. In one swift motion he removes my shorts, just now realizing I am not wearing any underwear. Surprise finds his eyes, "Fuck Quinn, do you have any idea what you do to me?"

"I know exactly what I do to you, because you do the same to me." My ability to form a coherent sentence is interrupted when the stubble on his chin meets the inside of my thigh.

"Oh God, Walker!" I scream out as his mouth meets my pulsing clit. He slides two fingers inside of me and I gasp. I want all of this man. I could live with him inside of me at all times, but as good as this feels right now it isn't enough. Knowing that his throbbing member is just inches away from me makes me crazy with lust. I can't take it. "Please, I want you inside of me." I am begging for him to fuck me.

"You got it, babe." With one fluid thrust, all of him is inside of me, and we are connected in a way that I have never felt. Not even last weekend.

No, this time is different, this time we have admitted our love for each other. He is taking it slowly, moving his hips in every direction, making sure to hit every spot inside of my core. Reaching between us, his fingers find my nub and squeezes, giving me the perfect amount of pain and pleasure to send me over the edge.

"Oh God, oh God, I'm going. Babe, I am going."

"I know, babe. I can feel your tight pussy squeezing my dick. It's incredible. I can't handle it." He grunts out as he empties himself into me.

"Shit" he exclaims after our bodies relax, and we both struggle to catch our breath.

"Yeah babe, shit." We lay there for awhile just holding on to each other, taking in everything that just happened.

"I love you."

He turns his head, looking deep into my eyes. "Not as much as I love you." Leaning up on his elbow he says, "Lets get cleaned up and get some clothes on before I take you again right here on the couch."

I giggle, "Would that be such a bad thing?"

He slaps my ass and stands up, "No, I guess not. But let's at least continue this in the bedroom where I can sprawl you out and do naughty things to you."

I let out a shriek as he picks me up, throwing me over his shoulder. With my bare ass sticking straight up in the air, he marches us towards the bedroom.

Chapter 17

Quinn

I wake to the sound of something vibrating, I blink a few times and look around the bright room.

Apparently, we were once again so into our dirty activities last night that we forgot to close the curtains. Good thing there are trees between my house and the neighbors, or they would be getting quite the show these days.

I hear the shower running, so I jump up and head in to join him. Just as I am about to open the door to the bathroom, I hear the vibrating noise again. Looking around the room, I spot Walker's cell phone on the dresser. It must be something important, because it is the second call in five minutes. I reach out to grab it and notice it says Amy on the screen, instantly my stomach sinks.

Why is Amy calling him? I send her to voicemail and the home screen pops up. Five missed calls from her this morning and many more texts messages. "Why didn't you call me last night?", "We need to talk about things if we are going to make this work, Walker!!", "I need to see you soon. This distance is killing me.", "I still love you, and I know you still love me." These are just the ones I can see. I swipe right on the screen to open it, fully aware that this is an invasion of his privacy, but I have to know.

Shit. He has a lock on his phone. Before I start jumping to conclusions, I try to remind myself that he told me about the lock because of the guys at work. At least, that's what his story was. Maybe he really is still talking with his ex fiance and wanted a reason for his phone to be locked so I couldn't see it.

I start replaying all of the moments in my head when he acted weird about his phone, and I just brushed them all aside like it was nothing. The morning after we had sex for the first time, and after he looked at his phone, his whole demeanor changed and he basically ran out the door. Or when we were making out outside of the salon earlier this week, and his phone was vibrating like crazy the entire time. He refused to pull it out to look at it. Instead he just ignored the buzzing, saying that he was sure that it was nothing. Then I come back to the lock on his phone. I get having it while he is at the station, but why keep it on all the time?

Now I have successfully worked myself into a complete frenzy. I hear the shower turn off. I have to make a quick decision- put the phone down and pretend I wasn't just snooping through it, or address it.

Fuck that, I am addressing this shit right now.

I pace back and forth wearing stress marks into the carpet until the bathroom door finally swings open. I turn to look at him, naked, except for the white towel wrapped around his waist. Damn, how am I supposed to have a serious conversation when he walks out looking like a Calvin Klein underwear model?

"Oh hey, babe. I hope I didn't wake you. I woke up and you looked so peaceful I didn't want to disrupt you, but I needed a shower. Seems my whole body was sticky from our ice cream adventures last night." He stalks towards me. "Totally worth it though. That shit was hot. Ok, well, maybe it was actually pretty fucking cold, but you know what I mean."

He leans in for a kiss, but I stop him by pulling back. If I am going to do this then I can't have his magic fucking lips on me. "Is everything okay, babe?" He asks with a questioning look.

"Do you and Amy still talk?" I barely get the words out. His face pales and he sheepishly looks at me like he is super guilty right now.

"No… why do you ask?"

"Because I woke up to your phone going off. And when I was on my way to join you in the shower I heard it go off again, so I wanted to make sure it wasn't something important." I let out a long breath, "But it was Amy, she has called a bunch of times and texted things that make it sound like you two have been talking"

"You went through my phone?" He asks. I can't quite read the expression crossing his face, but it is a mix of guilt and anger.

Wrong answer buddy.

"No, actually, I did NOT go through your phone. There is a passcode on it. But I did read the few texts that were up on the screen." I toss the phone into his hands.

He looks down at the screen, reading exactly what I read just minutes ago. He lets out a frustrated sigh, "No, Quinn, we aren't talking again. She has been calling and texting me non-stop since last Sunday. Before that, she would call or text about once a week, but I haven't answered or responded to anything. I'm not evening listening to her pathetic voicemails. I just keep deleting them."

"What does she want?"

"Well apparently you read them, so why don't you tell me? She says she wants to talk, she wants to make things better, that she misses me. Same shit over and over again." He runs his hands through his hair, obviously this is a conversation he doesn't want to be having right now. In the weeks that I have known him, we haven't once had a real conversation about Amy, other than him telling me that she cheated and he left. It is obvious this isn't a talk he wants to have, but too bad, we are having it.

"So Amy is the one who texted you last Sunday when you got all distant and ran out of here?" He nods. "Why couldn't you just tell me that, this looks bad, Walker. But if you were just upfront with me from the get-go, then I wouldn't be standing here second guessing us right now."

"Because, Quinn, it's really none of your business. Shit with Amy is in the past and that's exactly where I want to keep it." Breaking eye contact with me he heads over and starts getting dressed.

What is he doing? Is he really going to leave here right now? That doesn't work for me, I am more of the 'let's sit and hash this out so we can move on' kind of girl.

"Well, I don't think that's fair. If we are going to be together, then we need to be upfront and honest about our past. I want to know these things. I need to know these things."

He turns quick on his heels, shooting daggers at me with his eyes, "Oh, so when my past shows back up, we have to talk about it and work through it together. But the fact that you go to the cemetery for hours at a time, multiple times a week is just supposed to be ok. We don't need to talk about that?"

Tears build up in my eyes, and I try to blink them away. I will not cry. I will not cry. My voice shaky I say, "What are you saying?"

"I'm saying that you talk to Brett more than you talk to me." And there it is. Those unspoken thoughts that were constantly bouncing around in the back of my head. Always wondering if he really struggled with my "relationship" with Brett. Going to the cemetery isn't for him, it's for me. My family kept insisting that I talk through my emotions with someone, and instead of paying a shrink, talking out loud to Brett seems to help me.

I lose the battle between me and my tears. My whole body goes numb, a feeling that I am unfortunately very used to. I can't believe he just threw Brett in my face.

He steps closer to me, reaching up to wipe away the stream that is now flowing, but I step back. "No." I say, trying to gather myself. "You know the difference between my past and your past?"

I pause, waiting for him to answer but then decide he doesn't deserve the chance. I continue. "Your past is here. Still in the present, our present. And she is trying to weasel her way back into your future. My past though-" I swallow hard. "My past is exactly that. Brett isn't going to walk back through those doors and tell me he still loves me and wants me back. He's dead Walker. He's not coming back!"

His phone vibrates again, and I can see her name flash across the screen. "You should probably get that, and I think it's best if you leave. Maybe we can talk later when we have both calmed down." All of my beliefs about how to handle disagreements fly out the window. There is no chance of having an adult discussion right now, because between the blur of my tears, all I can see is red.

He grabs his keys, wallet, phone, and puts them all in his pocket. He shakes his head, sighing, as he makes his way over to me, lays a light kiss on my cheek, and walks out the door ... breaking my heart into a million pieces.

Chapter 18

Walker

"Shit, shit, shit…" I slam my hands on the steering wheel. I handled that completely wrong. Why the fuck did I just toss Brett at her like that? It honestly doesn't bother me that she goes to see him; if anything it has made things with us better, almost like she is gaining the closure with him she needs to move forward with us.

"Us." I say it out loud and sarcastically laugh. Maybe if I wasn't such an idiot then there would be a us but after the way I acted, I wouldn't blame her if she never spoke to me again. Even though she went through my phone, the anger isn't really about her, it just triggered some bad shit that happened with Amy.

She was constantly accusing me of cheating, always demanding to see my phone. Or I would catch her going through it when I was in the other room. The thing is, I had nothing to hide, so she never found anything. It was just the principle that she obviously didn't trust me even though I never gave her a reason not to. Looking back she was overcompensating and projecting her own sins on me. It should have been me insisting to look through her phone. Maybe then I would have saved myself the humiliation of walking in on the two of them bumping uglies in my own bed.

I pull into my driveway and I grab my phone out of my pocket to call Quinn. I have to make this better, explain to her why the idea of her going through my shit bothered me so bad. After one ring it goes straight to voicemail. I can't blame her, I was a major dick back there. I hang up and decide that sending her a text is a better idea than leaving a voicemail. At least, there is a better chance that she will see it.

Me: I'm sorry. I know what I said was hurtful and a low blow. Honestly I don't even feel that way about you going to the cemetery. I love you, Quinn. Please give me a chance to

make this right and explain to you what just happened.

Me: Please

I sit in my truck, stare at my phone, and wait, for what seems like hours. In reality, it was only a few agonizing minutes. Finally, the little bubble on the screen pops up, then disappears again. Fuck. I should just drive back over there and talk to her face-to-face.

Me: I'm coming back over, I need to talk to you.

The bubble instantly appears.

Quinn: No, please don't.

Me: I want to explain and apologize.

Quinn: I just need a little space right now. I'm not mad, mostly just hurt that you brought Brett into this. I never thought I would have to defend myself to you about going to go visit him. I thought maybe you were different. Actually, I know you are different, which is why this hurts so much. Let's just take the day to calm down, and I will meet you at Stubs tonight for JR's party.

I run my hands through my hair. Man I am such a dick. This woman was literally broken when I met her, and I busted my ass to put all of her pieces back together again yet here I am, breaking her even more. I have to make this better. My phone starts to vibrate, and without looking, I quickly answer, hopeful it's Quinn.

"Hey."

"Oh my god! You answered," Fuck. This is not the voice I was hoping to hear on the other end of the line. Damnit, Walker, why didn't you look at the screen before answering it? I contemplate hanging up, but decide that Amy is obviously not giving up as easily and I thought, so I just need to get this over with.

"Walker. Sugar, are you still there?" Ugh, sugar, I always hated when she called me that.

"Yep, I'm here. What do you want, Amy?" I step out of my truck and head inside before I decide to drive my sorry ass back over to Quinn's and beg for her to let me inside.

"Oh, sugar, I'm so glad you finally picked up, I knew you would come around eventually."

"Again, Amy, is there something I can help you with, or did you just call to remind me of the terrible pet name you thought I needed to have?"

She lets out a laugh as fake as she is, "Oh, Walker, you are so funny! I'm calling because I miss you, and I know you have to me miss. I need to see you, when can we meet up at talk?"

I walk over to the fridge and grab a beer. It may only be ten in the morning but if I am going to deal with this shit, I need a drink. "First off, you're wrong; I don't miss you. Not even a little actually. And second, you do realize I don't even live in Illinois anymore, right? So you seeing me is basically impossible."

"Yes, yes, I heard you moved to some small town in Michigan." I should be surprised that she knows this but considering she was blowing one or more of the guys on the department, I'm sure she has her ways of figuring shit out. "However, I'm willing to come to you. Today even. From what I understand, it is only about a three hour drive from here, I'll rent a car and be there in time for dinner."

"No!" I shout into the phone, as I begin to pace. "Dammit, Amy. We are done. DONE!" I take a deep breath, trying to calm myself so I can get the rest of this out. "There is no us anymore. Us ended the minute I walked in on you and my friend-my fire brother- fucking in my own damn bed."

"But Walkerrrrr…" she whines annoyingly. How did I ever find this behavior attractive? Quinn would never behave like this to get her way.

"Just stop and let me finish. I'm going to be really honest with you, and it isn't with the intention to hurt you. I met someone, a woman who has shown me what it feels like to really be in love. I don't think, actually, I know for a fact, that I was never in love with you. And I don't believe you really loved me either. It's just time to move on, Amy. I moved away and started a new life with new people. We don't even have to worry about running into each other. You can have Chicago and all of our friends there, but I need you to leave me alone. We are done. Now please stop calling me."

I stop for a second and listen to the other end of the phone. I can tell she is crying but girls like Amy are programmed from birth that it isn't ok to show emotion. So I know she won't try to speak until she has pulled herself together. I use this to my advantage, "Have a good life, Amy. I hope nothing but the best for you."

Then I hang up, hopeful that I just closed the door on that chapter of my life. What a relief!

My thoughts quickly go back to Quinn and I realize I never replied to her last text message.

Me: I'll see you tonight. I love you, Quinn, and I'm sorry for being such an asshole.

Chapter 19

Walker

Walking into Stubs tonight, my focus is on one person and one person only, my girl. It took everything in me to stay away from her house today like she asked me to. I have a lot of flaws, but I am the first to admit when I am in the wrong. I know that I screwed up.

After surveying the entire bar I come to the conclusion she has yet to arrive. I make my way over to JR, who is chatting with a bunch of the guys from the department. I throw my hand up in the direction of the bartender to get his attention and I order myself a beer and a round of celebratory shots for everyone. I have pretty much been drinking non-stop since that shitty phone call with Amy this morning. So, at this point, it is either stop and pass out, rally and get this party started.

Rally it is.

I slap JR on the shoulder, "Happy birthday, man."

He takes a long swig of his beer to wash down the tequila shot he just took, looks over at me, and then looks around. "Thanks, man. And, not that I'm not glad you're here, but where is your better half?"

"She's coming. I'm assuming she will show up with Halee." I barely finish the thought when her bubbly best friend walks through the door. My eyes are now locked on that same door hoping that Quinn will follow.

JR must be watching the same thing because he blurts out, "Huh. Well there's Hales." He looks at me with a pissed off look on his face. "What did you do?"

"Hey, guys. Where's Quinn?" Halee approaches us and scans the area. She makes brief eye contact with the bartender who must have signaled towards her normal because she nods and shoots him a flirty wink. "No, really, where is my girl? I have so much shit to talk to her about."

At this point they are both looking to me for answers, but I don't have any. She said she was going to be here. I pull out my phone to make sure she hasn't called or texted, but when I see my phone screen is still blank, I decide to send her a message.

Me: Hey, babe. Everyone is asking where you are. You are still coming, right? I miss you.

I wait a couple seconds to make sure she doesn't reply right away. Someone clearing his throat draws my attention. I shove my phone in my pocket and turn back to JR and Halee.

"You want to start by explaining why she didn't just come with you?" JR aggressively spits out like a loyal big brother would.

These people love her, and I get it, I love her, too. I look back and forth between the two of them and then I finally reply. "We got into a little fight today." I pause to gauge their reaction. "My crazy ex has been calling and texting me since I left Chicago, but it's has been basically non-stop for the past week."

Halee speaks up, "That's who texted you last Sunday when we were all at Quinns, wasn't it? I could tell something was up with you, your whole demeanor changed instantly when you looked at your phone." I give her a nod. "But what does that have to do with Quinn? I know my best friend, and she doesn't have a jealous bone in her body. Girls used to throw themselves at Brett when we were younger, and she would always just laugh it off."

I run my hands through my hair to the back of my neck where they form a tight grip. I could strangle myself for being such a dick. "Well, that isn't exactly why we are fighting." I empty my mug of beer and send the bartender a glance, pleading for another one. Quickly after I tell these two what I said to her, one of them is going to beat my ass. I would deserve it. If I was in their shoes, then I would want to take down anyone who hurt my girl the way I did this morning.

They wait impatiently as I take a swig of my fresh beer, deciding it's time to man up and tell them what I said. I know that I screwed up.

Fifteen minutes and a couple beers later, JR looks at me like he is out for blood, and Halee has tears in her eyes. Brett was important to these two, as well, so I'm sure my low blow hits them hard, just like it did Quinn. I pull my phone back out, only to see the same blank screen.

Me: Please, babe. If you aren't coming here, at least let me come to you. We need to talk. I need you so damn bad. PLEASE. Just answer me.

I glance back up and see the two of them looking at my phone. JR clears his throat, "Well, I suppose I don't have to beat your ass. From the looks of that text you're already beating yourself up pretty badly. Make this right, man. And I swear to God, if you ever throw Brett in her face like that again, I will personally make sure you don't walk again."

JR isn't as big as I am, and I definitely have about thirty extra pounds of muscle on him. But right now I know he could and would make good on his promise, if I fuck up again.

Halee sets her hand on my shoulder, tears still threatening the rims of her eyes. "You're a good man, Walker. More importantly, you are good for Quinn. If she said she will be here, then she will be. Knowing her she probably just needed a little space to wrap her head around everything. You screwed up, but she loves you." After giving me a sweet smile, Halee leaves and walks over toward a group of girls at the other end of the bar.

"How about some more shots?" JR yells to the group, and everyone hollers out in approval. He makes eye contact with me on his way back around to order, "You heard Hales, she'll be here. But until then, let's get drunk. It's my mother fuckin' birthday after all."

✄✄✄

I pull my phone out of my pocket and look at the time. Blinking a few times to clear my vision. It's ten thirty. Maybe I should slow down on the shots a little; I don't need to be falling over drunk when Quinn gets here.

If she gets here… the party started at eight. I contemplate trying to call or text her again, but all of my previous attempts have gone unanswered. So I decide to leave it alone. I have apologized and tried to make this better. If she wants to talk then she knows where I am; if not, then I will start groveling for her forgiveness again tomorrow.

"Dude, the hottest woman I have ever seen just walked in." JR slurs, "She definitely isn't from around here though, man. She is wearing sky high heels, and a dress like that should be illegal. You should see the rack on this chick. I am already imagining my head between those bad boys tonight. Happy Birthday to me."

I turn in the direction JR is pointing, reaching up to rub my eyes a couple times. I must really be drunk because I swear I have seen that head of hair before and those legs. The woman slowly turns in our direction, squinting around like she is looking for someone specific. My eyes make their way from her legs back up her body and stop to appreciate the set of twins JR was just raving about. When I get up to her face my stomach drops, "Oh fuck."

JR whips his head in my direction, "Oh, no you don't, asswhip! You already landed the hottest girl in town, and have the other ones falling all over you. Back off, this one's mine. What part don't you understand about me already picturing my head between those perfect titties?"

I let out a laugh, "Well, I can tell you one thing- they are perfect. Perfectly fake."

"Now how in the fuck could you possibly know those are fake from all the way across this dimly lit bar?" He snarls at me.

Now that she has spotted me, she makes her way in our direction, "I know because I helped pay for them."

"Hey there, sugar..." She drawls, giving me a flirty smile. Her voice is even more annoying in person. I turn to JR with a pleading look, hoping he doesn't leave me alone with her. Utter confusion spreads across his face while he turns his head back and forth between the two of us, trying to connect the dots in his drunken birthday head.

"What are you doing here, Amy?" I ask, still avoiding eye contact.

"Oh shit!" JR catches up to what's going on. "I'm going to go grab another beer. Good luck, bro." He slaps me on the back, laughing as he disappears.

Cool, thanks 'bro'. I finally direct my attention to the woman in front of me. The woman who, last time I saw her she was bent over my bed getting railed from behind by someone who was not me. I shake my head slightly to clear the memory.

Looking at her now, I notice all the things about her I never seemed to pay attention to before. The hair, nails, fake tits, her beauty isn't effortless like Quinn's. Everything about my ex fiancé is fake.

"I'm only going to ask you one more time. What are you doing here, Amy?"

She shifts uncomfortably and looks around probably thinking a place like this is beneath her. The only time she would go out in the city is if they had VIP seating and bottle service. God forbid we go to a dive bar to play pool and have a couple drinks. "Let's maybe go somewhere else and talk. This place is so… dark."

I look around and smile, this bar is filled with people I have come to care about. "Naw, I'm good here, but you are welcome to leave." I tip my beer in the direction of the door before bringing it to my mouth.

"Walkerrrr…" she whines. God this woman gets on my nerves. How in the hell did I manage to stay with her as long as I did? Anytime she doesn't get her way, she throws a fit like a toddler. In the past, I would give in, but not tonight. Not ever again. "I drove all the way here to see you the least you could do is talk to me." She reaches her hand up to touch my hair, but I tilt it in the opposite direction so it's out of reach. "Your hair is getting longer, I like it sugar."

"Don't." I take a step back but stumble a little. I try to control my anger, but the countless shots and beer I have had tonight doesn't weigh in my favor. "Don't touch me, Amy. If you have something to say, then say it. But I thought I made myself pretty damn clear this morning when I said that I am done. I have moved on. How did you even know I was going to be here tonight?"

She expertly flips her hair over her shoulders and gives a proud look, "Oh, those sweet men at that quaint fire house said you would probably be here for a friend's birthday." Shocker. She went to the firehouse. She also probably got down on her knees to show her appreciation before heading here. "Speaking of you moving on, where is this mystery girl? I would love to meet her."

"She isn't here and you're not going to meet her. But I'll tell you what you are going to do. You're going to get back into your rental car, drive your ass back to the city, and never contact me again. Sound good?"

It's like everything I just said went right over her head because instead of looking hurt, she looks at me like she just won the lottery. She braves coming within reach. Man I am too drunk to deal with her shit any longer.

"You mean to tell me that this woman, who supposedly stole your heart away from me, isn't out with you on a Saturday night? When you were mine, I never let you out of my sight." As her fingers trail up my shirt, I try to back up, but I run straight into a wall. "Come on sugar, just one more night. That's all I am asking for. Let me rock your world so you can remember how great we are together."

The alcohol must be impairing my reflexes because before I can react, her lips are on mine. She throws her body all over me, pinning me against the wall. I push her off but when I look across the bar, I realize I am too late. I see Quinn running out the door.

"Quinn!"

Chapter 20

Quinn

I have been wrestling with the decision about going tonight since my argument with Walker this morning. What he said to me really hurt, but I also know that he didn't mean it and only said those things out of anger. What I don't know is what made him so angry. Obviously me looking at his phone triggered something in him, but I don't understand what it is. I just wish he would have talked to me before exploding.

It's almost ten thirty when I finally pull myself up off the couch. I've been dressed and ready since seven, but I kept telling myself, just one more episode of Greys, and then I will go.

I pull into Stubs and instantly see his truck. I'm not sure why this makes my stomach drop, it's not like I didn't know he was going to be here. I've read all of his text messages and seen his missed calls. Halee even texted at one point telling me I'd better get my ass here before she comes and drags me out of the house.

So here I am walking in, when I would much rather have this conversation tomorrow. Because, judging by Walker's last text, he is already drunk.

Walker: u toming?

It's pretty obvious no real conversation will happen between us tonight, and I've never really been great at pretending everything is ok. But I walk through the door anyway.

I spot everyone at the bar instantly and make my way over. The only person who isn't standing there is the man I need to see the most. One smile from him and I'll know things between us are going to be fine. One smile, that's all I need.

"Hey, guys, what are you all staring at? Where is…" just as I'm about to finish that sentence, I see what they are looking at. Across the bar is a gorgeous woman with long, blonde, wavy hair, and judging by her revealing dress, it looks like she has a banging body. But what draws my attention more is what she is doing- pushing herself up against a man. My man. I stand there, frozen, watching this woman run her fingers up and down those abs I've gotten to know so well. It's like a bad accident you pass on the highway that you can't seem to pull your eyes from but you know you should.

She keeps leaning in when she says things. He looks like he is trying to lean back, but she has him pinned. "Who is she?" I break my focus away from them and look at Hales, her eyes filled with sadness. Has this woman been here all night? Why didn't anyone call me? "Halee, who the fuck is she?"

JR steps up behind me and says, "It's Amy." I return my attention back to what seems to be the show in the corner only to find her lips and hands all over him. Everything in me wants to run over there and rip those fake extensions out of her hair. But, before I make a fool of myself, I turn and run out the door.

"Quinn!" I hear his voice, but I don't stop. How could he do this to me? He brought her here and then basically begged me to come out tonight. Was this some sick joke? Get me to fall in love with him and then rip my heart out in front of everyone who means anything to me?

As I pull out my keys to get in the Jeep, I feel his strong hands on my elbow. He turns me around so we are face-to-face. I'm not able to hold back the tears this time. Walker gently cradles my face with his hands, and looks at me with pleading eyes, "Babe, wait. Please let me explain." I smell her perfume on him. My man smells like a woman who is not me.

My words come out more like sobs, "Explain what? Have you stayed in contact with her this whole time, Walker? Why? Why did you weasle your way into my life and my heart if you just planned on breaking it? Don't you think I have been through enough?" I wait for him to reply but when nothing comes. "Dammit, Walker! Say something!"

He backs away, breaking eye contact with me. "I didn't know she was coming here, and up until this afternoon, I hadn't talked to Amy since the day I walked out of our condo. Today when she called, I answered only because I thought it was you calling me back. I told her that she and I are done and have been done since I left. I told her I found someone who makes me feel things I never knew I could feel. I wished her the best, and then I hung up."

The old front door on Stubs squeeks open grabbing our attention. When we glance over, Amy is leaning up against the side of the building with a smug look on her face like this is a game, and she has already won. Walker looks back at me, then to her, and then back at me again. "Quinn, I don't want her. Even if I never had met you, I still wouldn't want her." He says loud enough so she can hear. Lowering his voice back down, "But maybe you are right; maybe I'm not right for you either." He reaches up and pulls at his hair, a sign he is struggling with what he is about to say. "You have been through more in this lifetime than anyone should have to deal with, and I just keep adding to that hurt and pain."

He starts walking towards his truck, but turns around suddenly, "I'm sorry, Quinn. I'm sorry for flipping out earlier over something that had nothing to do with you. I'm sorry I didn't tell you that she was calling and texting me. I hoped she would just go away if I ignored her. But, mostly, I'm sorry I even moved here. It's obvious your life would be better off without me in it."

As I listen to his words, it registers- he is breaking up with me, in a bar parking lot, after I just caught him with his ex's tongue down his throat. "Bullshit. You know what," he stops and turns around. "You are an asshole."

He lets out a laugh, a fucking laugh. What is funny about this? "Yeah, Quinn, I got that. Have a good life."

"Are you seriously going to just walk away from me? From us? So everything you said to me, was that just to what, get me in the sack? Well, great job. You know if fire fighting doesn't pan out, then maybe you should take up acting, because you definitely had me believing you loved me."

I hear an obnoxious laugh from behind me, "Oh, sweetie, look at yourself. He could never love someone like you."

I turn to really get a good look at her. There isn't anything real about this chick; her hair, nails, tits. I'm pretty sure her lips even have injections in them. I open my door, "You're absolutely right. Not if fake bitches like you are what he typically goes for." I shut the door, turn on my Jeep, and drive away, watching the man I thought could change everything disappear in my rearview.

Chapter 21

Walker

It's been three weeks since that night at Stubs. The only silver lining is that Amy left, and I haven't heard from her since.

I also haven't heard from Quinn. In all fairness, I haven't reached out to her, either. That whole night is kind of a blur. I remember bits and pieces of the argument out in the parking lot, but the rest of the night is a complete wash. The only detail that replays vividly in my mind is the sight of her driving away in tears. I'm not sure I will ever get that image out of my mind or forgive myself for being the reason behind her pain.

I woke up the next morning still fully dressed with shoes, lying on my bed. I found out at my next shift that Halee brought me home. It's so embarrassing.

I texted her to say thank you and to ask how Quinn is doing, but I never got a response. I get it-these are her people, and at the end of the day, I'm the outsider. I'm the outsider who royally fucked up.

At least JR is talking to me again. I'm pretty sure it is just because we are on the same shift, and he doesn't want shit to be weird. I know I should text her, but I told her I would walk away. Also, I really believe that if she didn't want it this way, then she would contact me. So as much as it kills me, I'm going to do my best to avoid the regular places she goes and leave her alone.

That means I need to find somewhere else to get my haircut. I'm in serious need and, the longer it gets, the more it just reminds me of her. I don't need any damn help in that department. Shit, just driving my truck brings back memories that instantly get me hard.

We both jump into the cab of the truck through the passenger side. The rain is coming down so hard I can barely even see out the windshield.

"Holy shit! I guess we should have looked at the radar before we decided to go for that hike." I hear her talking but all I can focus on are her nipples because they look like they are about to rip through her soaked white t-shirt.

"Hey, mister, my face is up here." She gives me a light slap on the arm.

"Sorry, but damn, am I glad you chose to wear white today! Are you even wearing a bra right now?"

She gives me her typical Quinn eye roll, "Yes, Walker, I am wearing a bra. Well, sort of, it's called a bralette."

"Well, whatever it is, I definitely approve." I say as I pull her over onto my lap, making sure to place her just right so she can feel exactly what her body does to me.

"Ohh.... Mr. McCoy, do you have something in your pocket?"

I shake my head slowly, taking her all in, "MmmmMmmm. No ma'am that is all me." She bites down on her lip, driving me wild as I lift up her shirt, taking her fake bra with it. "I think these nipples are begging for some attention from my lips." I pull them one by one into my mouth using my teeth. She arches her back and begins grinding her hips down into me. I can feel the heat radiating from her pussy as I slowly rid her of her jean shorts and moist panties.

"Well, this seems entirely unfair. Once again, here I am completely naked and you are still fully clothed. I think we need to change this." She pulls at the hem of my shirt but struggles due to its wetness. So I reach behind my head and pull it off by the neck. She starts unbuckling my belt and unbuttoning my cargo shorts. I lift my hips as she slides them down to about mid thigh. Even if it wasn't down pouring outside, the steam from our heavy breathing on the windows would protect us from any outside eyes.

At first I just nibble at her lip, but she lets out the sexiest little cry. So I insert my tongue and dominate her mouth the way I know drives her crazy. She runs her hands through my hair, pulling just slightly and then lets them roam along my neck and back. The way she touches me is the same as it always is, like this could be her last time.

I cup her tight ass to lift her hips just enough so I can align my dick under her dripping slit, then slowly I lower her down on top of me. Both of us moan, intensifying the dance our tongues are doing. We grind on each other until I can tell she is as close as I am. I reach my hand down between us and start rubbing and squeezing her clit the way I know she loves.

Within a few seconds, her whole body responds to me.

"Oh god, Walker, I am so close!" she screams. People may not be able to see us but I'm sure they can hear her.

"I know. Me too. I can feel you squeezing me." I grunt between breaths. We give each other every ounce of energy we have left. Then we just sit here, still connected and feeling each other's heartbeats steady back to normal.

"If we stay like this much longer, I am going to get hard again." I start to move her off of me.

She grips tighter around my neck and whispers, "That doesn't sound like a bad thing, let's go with that."

I move her over to the side and use my shirt to clean her up. When I look back up at her, she is sporting her best pouty face. "Once we get back to the house, we can do whatever you want. But the rain has let up, and I'm afraid if we stay here we might draw a crowd. You're not exactly quiet when you are screaming my name." I give her a wink, hand her clothes to over to her, and pull my shorts up.

The sound of our station's tone wakes me out of my fantasy. Once again I run towards the bay, trying to adjust my boner. Looks like I might have to sell my truck after all, because I can't be reminded of this shit every time I get in it.

Chapter 22

Walker

I know it goes against all of my training to take off my mask while inside a structure fire. But, if I didn't, then she was going to die. The woman had already been lying there, struggling to breathe, for who knows how long when I found her.

She has kids, who were already safely outside, and they need their mother. That alone was driving me harder, and I knew I could get us back outside in time without my mask; and I did. But that's the last thing I remember before I woke up in this damn hospital bed with tubes in my nose and JR's ugly mug staring at me.

I cough a little, clearing my soot coated throat, and JR's head snaps up from his phone. "Quinn." I manage to spit out. I could really use some water, so I reach toward the side table where a glass sits.

"Fuck, dude, let me get that for you. Man, am I glad you are awake! You scared the shit out of me. I was just about to run back in and find your stupid ass when you walked out and then collapsed in my arms." He hands me a glass of water, and I take a small drink.

"Leave it to you to make this shit about you, JR." I take another drink and clear my throat the rest of the way. "Can you do me a solid and call Quinn? If this shit has taught me anything, it's that I want her. No, I need her, and I am going to make damn sure she knows it. She isn't going to make decisions that she thinks are best for us without my input. We are meant to be together."

"Yeah, yeah, save your sappy speech for your girl. I'll call her, but I have to step outside. I don't have shit for service in here." He walks to the door, "I'll be right back, and I'll give the nurses a heads up that your needy ass is awake." He turns back around before walking through the door, "But really, man, I'm glad you're good."

I know seeing me go down like that must have been hard on a lot of these guys. They lost one of their own not long ago. And the look in JR's eyes tells me that no matter how pissed off he was at me for what happened with Quinn, he and I are friends. "Yeah, bro. Me too."

Very shortly after he walks out, two nurses run to my bedside, asking me how I am feeling and finding every excuse in the book to touch me. One even said she needed to check my abdomen, which seemed sketchy but I shrugged and let her examine me. "How soon can I get out of here?" Before either nurse can answer, a tall older man who introduces himself as Dr. Nelson, walks in and runs through the remainder of the exams. He explains that as long as my oxygen level stays where it is for the next two hours, then I should be out of here by noon at the latest.

JR makes his way back to my room just as the good doctor and the touchy nurses walk out. One of them turns around and says, "If you need anything, and I mean ANYTHING, please don't hesitate to hit the call button. I will be right down the hall. It's really no problem. In fact, it would be my pleasure." She gives me a flirty wink and walks out.

"What the hell is so funny?" I ask JR, who is sitting back in his chair laughing.

"You. I swear, you are in a god damn floral hospital gown looking like shit and still have all the ladies throwing themselves at you. It must be hard being you."

I wave my hand in the air dismissing his ridiculous comment, "There is only one woman I am interested in. Speaking of, did you get ahold of her?"

"I didn't. I tried, but her phone kept going straight to voicemail. I left her a message telling her to call me, but just in case I don't have service, I also called Hales to have her try to get ahold of Quinn."

A wave of disappointment hits me, and it must be obvious because he gets up and puts his arm on my shoulder, "Don't worry, man, she'll be here."

Ugh, the last time he said that to me was one of the worst nights of my life.

✂✂✂

I don't know what else to do, so I just keep looking at the clock. It's damn near one in the afternoon now, and the doctor started my discharge paperwork over an hour ago.

Quinn never showed up. I sat here and burned a hole in the clock on the wall for the past six hours. JR has tried calling her at least a dozen more times, and now even Halee isn't answering.

She obviously doesn't want to see me, and that shit hurts. I know we got into a serious fight, and we both said a lot of crap we didn't mean, but if she was the one sitting in a hospital bed, it would take an army to keep me from her. I assumed she felt the same way, but I must've been wrong.

In my mind I start to justify that maybe she isn't here because it's too hard. Maybe she's worried that seeing me in a hospital bed because of a fire will remind her of Brett, and it's just too much for her to handle. But as I run through all the possibilities of why she wouldn't want to be by my side, when less than a month ago she confessed her love for me, I stop myself. Fuck that, this may be hard on her, but this is hard on me. I need my fucking woman by my side.

A little voice in my head that sounds an awful lot like Amy, tells me "Quinn Harris isn't your woman anymore, remember? You told her you were better off apart'.

Shit. As soon as I get the "ok", I am out of here. The doctor walks in, goes over some paperwork, and tells me he wants me to get checked out by my regular physician in a week to make sure there isn't any permanent damage to my throat or lungs. I don't have a regular physician in Iron City, but I need to get out of here.

"So, I'm good? I can go?" I jump up off the bed, already dressed in the clothes one of the guys from the station dropped off. "JR, can you take me to my truck at the station? I gotta get out of here."

He stares at me in confusion, waiting for me to explain, "What do you mean, 'you gotta get out of here'? Where exactly are you going?"

"I don't know, man. Somewhere. Anywhere. I don't think I can stay in this town with her in it. Everywhere I look reminds me of Quinn. Maybe I will take that leave the chief offered me and just drive until it feels right to stop." He doesn't respond until we get to his truck.

"I get it, man, but I just think you leaving is a mistake. You guys are good together. Maybe she just needs time to work through this shit in her head. It must have hurt like hell for you to throw Brett in her face and then seeing Amy all over you. It's just going to take a little time."

"That's not the point, I needed her today. I needed her to put aside all the shit we both said and come to the fucking hospital. But, obviously, she doesn't give two shits about me, so that's cool. All I'm saying is I can't stay here and pretend to move on, or watch her move on with someone else eventually. I'm out. This is her town, and her people."

He doesn't say anything else the rest of the drive, so once we get to the station, I jump out and shut the door. I'm not good with goodbyes, and there's no way in hell we are going to hug it out. I hear him roll down the window and yell, "Just make sure your dumbass calls me when you figure out what the fuck you are doing. It matters to me, too."

I turn back to him, giving him a nod and smile.

And I drive away.

But something inside me won't let me leave just yet. There is one place I have to go- to visit the man whose shoes I've been trying to fill from the moment I arrived.

Chapter 23

Quinn

Why do I always thinks it's such a great idea to drink away my pain? Once again, I wake up hungover in my bed with sheets I refuse to wash because I keep telling myself they smell like him. I'm wearing one of the shirts and pairs of boxers he left here. It's probably pathetic, but it brings a sense of closeness that I don't feel otherwise.

After our blow up at Stubs, we haven't talked, which means everything he left at my house before that is still here. Most of it has been packed away in a box and shoved to the back of the hallway closet. The only things I kept out is what I am currently wearing, and the shirt still has his musky male scent on it. I'm ashamed to admit to anyone that I sleep in it every night. I dream about him, and the way he touched me. Some mornings I wake up to my fingers rubbing my clit, sending me into an orgasm because I dream they are his hands.

When my parents, Halee, or JR ask if I am ok, I respond with a nod and a smile, but I'm not ok. I thought losing Brett was the biggest heartbreak I would ever experience, but I was wrong. Knowing that the man who owns your heart is just miles away but wants nothing to do with you, tops the cake. Some days, I even hate going into work because now, instead of women looking at me with sympathy over my fiance dying, some have the balls to ask if I would be offended if they went after Walker.

I lean over and grab my phone to see the time, but it's dead. Cool, apparently when my drunken body stumbled into bed last night, plugging it in wasn't a priority. Way to go, drunk Quinn.

Who would need to call me anyway? I wonder as I plug it in and head to the closet. I have way too much on my mind to sit around the house today. It won't be fun with a hangover but going for a run to sweat this booze out of my system and clear my mind is exactly what I need.

✂✂✂

Shit, it's still so hot for late August. I think I started sweating the minute I stepped outside and now, after a five mile run, I am drenched. I strip off my tank top, sports' bra, and jogging shorts, depositing them in the hamper on the way to the shower. Shortly after putting shampoo in my hair, I hear a pounding noise that sounds like it is coming from my front door.

It doesn't let up by the time I'm done rinsing it out. So I step out, dripping wet, and wrap my robe around me. As I get closer to the door, I hear Hales screaming for me to open up. She sounds upset.

When I open the door, I can see her eyes are glossed over, like she is going to cry or already has been. I can't quite tell which. "Hales, come in. What's wrong? And why didn't you use your key to let yourself in?"

"Where the hell is your phone at Quinn?" She screams, ignoring my question. "I have been calling you since five this morning, but I was up at my parents cabin so I couldn't get to town until now." She gasps for air like she hasn't taken a breath in hours. "You have to get dressed, Quinn, we need to get to the hospital."

Confused I look at her and start heading towards my room, "Hospital? Halee what are you talking about? And my phone died sometime throughout the night, apparently I never plugged it in."

She grabs my shoulders and jerks me around, "Quinn, look at me… there was a structure fire last night."

My heart stops.

Structure fire.

Hospital.

My mind tries to register what she is saying to me.
Oh god, Walker.

"From what I understand he is alive. But he was on a rescue team and got separated from the others. He came across the person they were looking for, so he removed his face mask so the woman would have oxygen. They both made it out safely, but he collapsed as he was walking through the door."

My ears stop listening after the words 'he is alive' are spoken and my heart rate slows back down. He is going to be ok. He has to be ok. I can't lose him, too, especially not like this. "Halee, he has to be ok. I can't..." I squeak out as my tears break through. My whole body shakes when she pulls me into her arms. "Halee, I can't lose him, too."

She releases me from her hold and move me in the direction of my room. "He woke up after they got him to the hospital this morning, and he was asking for you. JR called me when he couldn't get through to your phone. When you weren't answering me, I jumped into my parents car because they were blocking mine in. That's why I don't have your house key with me. There was an accident near Grand Rapids, so I was stuck in traffic for what seemed like forever. I'm sorry, I tried to get here as soon as I could."

I turn from her to start dressing, and one of the first things I see, ironically enough, is his shirt I wear every night. Dressing as quickly as I can, I practically run out the door without shoes before Halee tells me to put on some flip flops. He has been at the hospital asking for me since before six o'clock this morning, and it is now two in the afternoon. "I'm coming, babe." I say to myself, praying he somehow hears me, and feels my love.

But it's been eight hours, he probably thinks that I don't want to see him. Shit. Why couldn't my drunk ass remember to plug in my phone last night? I swear I am never drinking again. "Quinn!" Halee yells from behind me, "Why don't you ride with me? You don't need to be driving right now."

She's right, we don't need both of us laid up in the hospital. That is exactly what would happen, too, because there is absolutely no way I would be stopping at any of the lights on the way there. I change direction toward her parents car, "Yep, good idea. Drive fast, Hales. I need him."

"I know, sweetie. We will hurry. Safely." She gives me a sympathetic smile that tells me everything is going to be ok.

It has to be ok.

Chapter 24

Quinn

I carelessly sprint into the hospital, almost knocking over an older lady using a cane. "I'm so sorry." I yell on my way by. When I finally make it to the nurse's station, I struggle to catch my breath, "I'm. Here. To. See. Walker. McCoy." I finally get out, wheezing in between each word.

The woman behind the desk shows zero emotion or concern as she looks at me over her super thick glasses. Then she shifts her eyes down to her screen, and just as I am about to ask if she is deaf, she says, "Looks like you just missed him. He checked out about thirty minutes ago."

I pivot on my heels and spot Halee just walking in the door, she went to park the car after dropping me off at the entrance. I run in her direction, grab her arm and yank her in the opposite direction with me. "Jezz, Quinn! What's going on?"

"He's not here, Hales. He checked out thirty minutes ago. And I left my phone sitting on the nightstand at home. I was too worried about getting to him to even think about grabbing it. Damnit, now what do I do?"

She pulls her phone out of her back pocket and calls someone, "Hey, JR. Yeah, sorry, my phone fell under my seat at some point during the drive from the cabin, and I was too worried about getting to Quinn that I never stopped to grab it." She pauses for a second, "What do you mean he is leaving town?" Her worried eyes shift to me.

I don't even hesitate before I grab the phone out of her hands, "Who is leaving town? JR. What the hell are you talking about?"

"Shit, Quinn, he waited for you all day! That man stared at the clock for hours, and anytime someone walked into the room, he got excited thinking it was you. When you didn't show, he took that as you didn't want to see him. He said that he can't stay here in Iron City and pretend he doesn't love you while watching you move on with someone else. He took a leave of absence from the department and said he was just going to drive until it felt right."

"How long ago did he leave?" I can physically feel my heart breaking in two. But the pain in my chest is probably nothing compared to what Walker felt today, while he sat and waited for me. And I didn't show. "I have to fix this, JR. When did he leave?"

"Probably twenty minutes ago. But, Quinn, he left his phone here at the station, and I have no idea where he was going. I'm not even sure he knew. I'm so sorry, I tried to talk him out of it."

"I gotta go. Please have him call Halee's phone, if he comes back." Then I hang up.

I look over at Halee, her pained expression and tears match mine. I can't let him leave without knowing how much he truly means to me. He is everything. "Take me to his house, Hales. Maybe he stopped there before he heads out of town." I mumble that I can't lose him under my breath as I turn to look out the car window. She doesn't say anything; she just sets her hand on top of mine and squeezes.

Why am I so stubborn? I should have made this right weeks ago. Instead, I stuck my head in the sand and pretended I didn't want him anymore. When the truth is, I don't think I've ever wanted anything more in my life. Of course, I wanted Brett. But that was more about the natural progression of things after being together for so long. This is different. I need Walker like I need oxygen. Damn you, stubborn Quinn.

We are coming up on the cemetery, and I can't help but think about what Brett would tell me right now. He would most likely laugh and say something like 'Yeah, I could've told you that you are stubborn as shit' or something else irrelevant in an effort to make me smile. Looking out my window in the direction of his grave, my eyes find a black truck. Not just any black truck, Walkers black truck. "Stop the car!" I yell, and Halee slams on her breaks.

"Quinn. What the hell? You scared the shit out of me!" But I don't stick around to answer. Instead I throw off my seat belt, and I'm out the door in seconds, sprinting towards the only two men who have ever owned my heart. Why they are together is still a mystery.

I see Walker standing with his back to me, looking down at Brett's grave. As I get closer, I can hear his voice...

"Hey, man. I don't really know why I'm here. But for some reason I couldn't leave this town without talking to you." In typical Walker fashion, one of his hands is running through his messy hair and the other is pulling on his neck.

"I feel like the worst person in the world because there have been so many moments over the past few months that I was grateful you didn't make it out of the fire that day. I know it sounds terrible, but if you were alive, I would've never joined the ICFD, and I would've never met Quinn."

He stops and lets out a long breath. "She is amazing, but you know that already. I'm so jealous of the years and memories you shared with her. I thought that she was it for me because she was the woman I saw my future with."

"We had a structure fire last night," he laughs, "but you already know that too, don't you? I wasn't sure if I was going to make it out, and all I could picture was Quinn's face. I know that if I died the same way you did, then she wouldn't ever bounce back from it. But she never came today. And damn, man, I needed her to come to the hospital like I need my own breath. So I think that's my sign to walk away. I never deserved a woman like her anyways. Her heart is so pure and I'm just an asshole. She deserves to spend the rest of her life with someone like you."

His voice goes flat, and I can tell he is trying to hold it together until he can get the rest of his speech out. "That's right, as much as it kills me to admit, you're the better man. I've known this from the minute I learned about you, but I tried to ignore it."

He fails to hold it back. I hear him sniffle, and his shoulders shake a little. I should let him know I am here, but I can't; I need to hear what he has to say.

"Look out for her, okay? I'm sure I don't have to ask, but I'm going to anyway. I love her and I will probably always love her. But I can't stay here and watch her move on with her life without me in it. She deserves to be happy."

I step towards him, "You make me happy."

He whips his body around, looks at me, and opens his mouth to speak. I walk over and put my finger on his lips, "Hold on, it's my turn to talk."

"You make me crazy happy." I wait, to give him a second to let that soak in. "I am so sorry I wasn't there for you today. My phone died in the middle of the night and was turned off and plugged in for majority of today. I didn't know what was going on until about a hour ago when Halee practically broke down my front door. We went straight to the hospital but they had said you were gone. Then JR told me you were leaving town? You can't leave. All those things you just said, I feel them, too. I love you. I want a future with you. I want to marry you and someday have babies with you." He smiles and raises his eyebrows at me. "Don't get cocky, McCoy. I'm not done yet. I should have made this better three weeks ago after Halee explained everything that happened that night at Stubs, but I'm stubborn."

I look down at Brett's grave and laugh, "He would tell you that. He always said I am the most stubborn girl in the world. Are you sure you want to put up with me? Because I guarantee you that I will challenge you daily. But I also promise that I will love you with everything I have. The idea of falling in love again didn't seem possible until I met you. You were my game changer, Walker McCoy. I love you so much, and, if you leave Iron City, then I'm leaving with you."

That cocky smirk has now transformed into his brilliant smile. "You done yet, woman? Is it ok if I talk now?" I nod, "I'm not going anywhere, babe. As long as you are here and you want me, I'm yours."

We embrace and within seconds are pulling at each other and kissing like it's the first or maybe even the last time. Minutes go by and we don't stop until Walker feels something on his left shoulder.

Bird poop.

He looks back at Brett's grave, laughs and brings his eyes back to mine. "I'm not sure if that is him giving his blessing, or if he is telling me to stop groping his girl right in front of him."

I can't help but smile. "Knowing him, I'm going to assume it's a little bit of both. Why don't we head home?" I walk over, place my hand on the headstone, and look up. A single tear falls down my face as I mouth the words 'Thank you' into the sky. I close my eyes and take in this moment.

I will never forget Brett Rhodes. He was the boy who first stole my heart and turned into a man right in front of my eyes. He promised to love me forever, and he died a hero.

When my eyes find Walker, he's leaning up against his truck a few feet away, giving me the space he knows I need. That man was sent to me when I needed him the most. He took all of my broken pieces and put them back together again.

Some people go their entire lives and never truly feel like they found their person, their soulmate, their happy place. I don't know how I got lucky enough to have two great loves in my life, but I will forever cherish and be grateful for both of them.

I kiss my hand, place it on the top of the head stone, and start making my way towards a smiling Walker. It's not just any old happy smile, it's his fuck me smile.

He holds out his hand as he opens the door and helps me in, then walks around the truck but never breaks eye contact with me. "So, I have a couple questions before we go."

"Shoot."

"When you say home, are you good with that being our home? Because I don't know if I am physically capable of spending another night without you if I don't have to."

I smile, "Yeah, babe. Our home. The only reason you get to sleep in another bed is if you are on shift. As far as I'm concerned our forever starts today."

He leans forward and places a gentle kiss on my nose, "Perfect, one more question."

Rolling my eyes, "I'm waiting, McCoy."

"How soon are you thinking about starting this whole baby thing? Because, I'm not going to lie, the idea of you carrying my child, makes me want to go all caveman on you and put one in there now."

God, this man. I have said it once and I will say it forever, he owns my heart.

"We should definitely go home and start practicing, so, when we are ready, we'll basically be professionals."

He puts the truck in drive and pulls out of the cemetery, "Yeah, babe. Let's go home."

Epilogue

Walker
One year later...

"Come on, babe. We are dying of thirst out here."

This past year has been like a dream- the girl, the job, the friends, and now the house. Quinn struggled with the fact that we were still living in the same home she and Brett used to share. Even though it didn't bother me, I understood why she needed a change.

So after about a week of looking, we found this perfect three bedroom house that Quinn said 'Will be perfect to raise a family in'. I love how open she is about talking about having kids, but in reality I think that she was most excited about the inground pool in the backyard. We have barely been here a week, and she has already invited all of our friends and her parents over for a cookout.

It actually works out in my favor because I've had this ring in my sock drawer for weeks, waiting for the perfect moment to pop the question.

That day after the cemetery, we went home and made love... multiple times. Then we cleaned ourselves up and she took me over to meet my soon-to-be-in-laws. I would be lying if I said that didn't intimidate the shit out of me, but they accepted me the second we met. And when I asked her dad's permission to propose a couple of months ago, he replied with 'I think you are the perfect man for the job'.

I walk through the slider with a tray of margaritas, "It's about time! Shit, did you have to run to Mexico for that tequila?" Halee. She never lets me down with her one-liners. She is here alone today because 'Mr. Right Now' didn't seem to pan out this time. I really don't get it; she is an attractive woman, down to earth, and easy to get along with, but for some reason she can't seem to get it right when it comes to men.

I hand everyone their drinks but Quinn, leaving one sitting on the tray next to a little black box.

She looks down and registers what is sitting right in front of her, and when her beautiful, emerald eyes find mine, I am already down on one knee. She lets out a gasp, along with all the other women on the deck, and she isn't even trying to hold her tears back. I clear my throat, "Quinn."

Her voice and body are shaky, "Yeah, babe."

"I feel like I have been waiting my entire life to find someone like you. I know I wasn't your first love, and I'm ok with that. But I'm kind of hoping that I can be your last. Will you marry me?"

"Yes!!! Yes, I will marry you! I love you so much Walker McCoy!"

"I love you, too, Quinn Harris. Today, tomorrow, and every day after that."

The End

For now... *wink face*

Acknowledgments

Where do I even start? I guess the beginning is a good place...

Hilary, thank you! Who would've ever thought when we sat down at drunk lunch that Monday afternoon, your crazy idea of me writing a book would lead to this.

My husband. Beau, your support means everything. You not only deal with my constant ramblings about characters that only exist in my head but you also encourage me to dream big and chase those dreams with everything I have. You are my rock, my heart and my biggest supporter. Thanks for doing life with me babe.

My girls aka my sounding board... I never would've gotten through this first book without you. Heck I don't think I would have made it this far in life without you guys. Writing about Quinn and Halee's friendship was easy when I know exactly what it feels like to have best friends that really feel like your sisters. Jord, Rae and Jess- thank you for putting up with my late night texts, listening to my ideas, telling me when you loved it and especially telling me when you didn't.

My beta readers. Jodi, Tammy & Brandy... I appreciate you guys and the honest feedback you gave me, more than you know.

The real MVPs who edit my crazy. Tammy and Kristen, you two are rockstars. Thank you!

Mom & Dad- thanks for always being in my corner and believing in my wild adventures. I love you.

Most importantly, anyone who is reading this. Thank you for your support. I typically don't throw myself into anything unless I know I'm going to be great at it. The idea of putting myself out there with the chance of failing, terrified me. So if you've supported me and my dream by purchasing this book, please know that I appreciate you.

Walker & Quinns Playlist

You Should Be Here - Cole Swindell
Drunk Me - Mitchell Tenpenny
Take Your Time - Sam Hunt
I Drive Your Truck - Lee Brice
Torn - Natalie Imbruglia
Something To Talk About - Bonnie Raitt
Never Be The Same - Camila Cabello
My Girl - Dylan Scott
God Gave Me You - Blake Shelton
Hangin' On - Chris Young
You Make It Easy - Jason Aldean
Bless The Broken Road - Rascal Flatts
Broken - Lifehouse
Too Close - Next

Iron City Heat Series

Someone Like You
(Walker & Quinn)

Someone Like Me
(Luke & Halee)

Coming Soon:

Someone Like Her
(Graham & Lennox)

Connect with Brit.

Instagram:
Instagram.com/Brit_Huyck

Facebook:
facebook.com/authorbrithuyck

Facebook Reader Group:
Brits Book Babes

Goodreads:
goodreads.com/author/Brittni_Huyck

Turn the page for a sneak peek of....

Someone Like Me

Prologue

Have you ever been in love?

Like the overwhelming, all consuming, mind numbing good love?

When you find the one that you know you want to spend the rest of your days with. It's the only person you can't imagine not falling asleep and waking up next to.

The one individual that you know was made for you… your soulmate, your other half, your rock, the love of your life.

Not many people get to really feel the intensity of finding the exact person that was created for them. Then getting to spend eternity making memories and just truly living.

I feel bad for these people.

I feel bad that they will never know what it feels like to look into someone's eyes and see forever staring back.

Fortunately for them, they will also never have to feel the pain of finally finding their person, only to watch them walk away. Taking their heart and every ounce of their colorful outlook on life with them.

As I sit here, a broken shell of the person that I once knew, I can't help but think… maybe they're the lucky ones.

Chapter 1

Halee

Four months earlier... May

I'm currently sitting across the living room from my best friend, who continues to gush over her seemingly perfect fiancé. All while we're supposed to be talking about their future wedding plans. This isn't bitterness in my voice. I'm truly happy for her, she deserves all the happiness in the world after everything she's been through.

Quinn was once in love and engaged to another man, her high school sweetheart, but everything changed the day he ran into a structure fire. He never came back out. I shouldn't be jealous of her, I know this. No one should ever have to endure the amount of pain and heartache she has.

My envy doesn't come from her pain.

It stems from the fact that she has not only had one great love, but two.

A year ago, I never thought anyone or anything would bring her out of the destructive state she was in after Brett died, but then came Walker. His six-foot-two body covered in muscles and tattoos came strolling into town. Just like that, everything in her world was right again.

I know people say that things happen for a reason, and it seems super shitty to think Brett died so she could meet Walker. But I think that's exactly what happened. She has a lightness about her now that I'd never seen with Brett, almost like things come easier for the two of them and the world is spinning exactly as it should be. Two soul mates found their way to each other, and here I am, on like relationship number one hundred and I can't seem to find a decent guy to save my life.

Over the years it feels like I have tried just about everything to meet a good guy. Even those crazy dating apps where you swipe left or right depending on what you are looking for. That was a joke, the only thing those guys were looking for was a quick lay and then they moved onto the next willing participant.

I don't feel like I have unrealistic expectations, a nice guy, family and goal oriented, active, someone who can make me laugh, doesn't take life too seriously and most importantly, can have a good time. But date after date that I go on just continues to be a let down.

The guy I was out with last week asked me to come back to his place so we could hang out and get to know each other better, but informed me as we were walking out of the restaurant that we had to keep it down because his mom is a light sleeper.

Thanks, but no thanks.

This all led me here, giving up on the idea of any near future relationships and accepting my role as the permanent third wheel to these two love birds.

"You two are annoyingly cute. I think I'm going to take off before I become even more depressed about my current lack of a love life."

Quinn peels her attention away from Walkers face and gives me a look of sympathy, "Sorry, Hales. I've been meaning to ask, how did your date last week go? You said that he seemed promising."

I let out a laugh remembering the look on that guys face when I told him I was suddenly experiencing explosive diarrhea and had to head home. "He was promising on paper and the date was great. In fact, he was basically ready for me to move in with him… and his mother. I faked a case of diarrhea and got out of there before he could ask about another date. Honestly I've been ignoring his calls since."

Walker laughs and looks up from whatever wedding pamphlet Quinn had him looking at, "You mean to tell me that you told this man you had a case of the shits, and he called you for a follow up?"

His hysterical belly laughing continues as Quinn chimes back in, "Yea Hales, maybe he is a decent guy."

"He absolutely IS a decent guy, but he also lives with his mother. And not because she's ill or because he needed a place to stay until he could get back on his feet. He straight up told me, 'It's like having a roommate that cooks for you and does your laundry'. No thank you, that's asking for trouble. I want an independent man who can take care of himself, not someone who will instantly be expecting me to take the place of his mother. Or worse, move in with the two of them so she can do my laundry and cook for me." Although looking back at the idea, I guess I can see the perks.

I wave my hand at them, "Anyways, I've decided to take a step back from the dating scene and focus on me for awhile. Maybe I've just been trying too hard and putting too much energy into finding someone. But enough about me, let's get back to this wedding planning. What's next on the list?"

Quinn's face lights up and she looks over to Walker and then back to me, slightly jumping up and down in her seat. "I've actually been meaning to talk to you about that, Walker has a friend that's a country singer. He's playing about two hours from here this weekend at a bar, I want to go check him out and see if he has the right feel for what we are looking for, but Walker can't go. He's covering a shift for one of the guys at the department. Soooo... I was thinking maybe we can make it a girls' night? You, me and Charlie?"

"Why can't you guys be normal and have a DJ like everyone else in the world?"

They both look at me as if I've grown two heads. After I realize that I would not be getting a reply I say, "Sure, count me in, but you better mention it to Charlie so that she can find a babysitter for Tuck."

"Already taken care of, JR offered to hang out with him for the night." Walker says. "He has a serious hard on for that girl, I'm pretty sure he would hang himself by his dick in the middle of winter if she'd asked."

Quinn rolls her eyes and elbows him in the ribs, "Ugh, why can't you just say that he likes her? That is such a gross visual. Plus I've told him over and over, she isn't ready to jump into another relationship right now."

When we hired Charlie we didn't know much about her, just that she was new to town, and looking for a fresh start. It wasn't until weeks later that we found out she has a three year old son named Tucker. She'd left southern Indiana because she was running from her piece-of-shit ex who used to hit her. She endured a lot being with him but one day he took it to the next level, laying his hands on Tuck. Charlie called the police and while he was at the station being questioned, she packed up everything she could fit in her car and left.

"I think she could, he just has to give her time. I can't imagine trying to trust someone and let them in after what that asshole put her through." I pause, "Back to our girls' night, tell me about this band. Walker, you know them?"

"Yea." He says as he stands up, heading to the kitchen. "You two want a drink?"

After we nod, he goes on, "Not really a band, just a single guy, his name is Luke. We met a few times in Chicago while I was living there. Super cool dude and seriously talented. He's from the south originally, at least I think, he has quite the southern drawl going on. I already know he's perfect but you know how miss has to control everything gets." He turns his thumb in Quinn's direction and she returns his gaze by sticking her tongue out.

Leaning down he hands us our drinks and kisses Quinn on the forehead. She lets out a dramatic scoff, "I do not need to control everything but the band is a big deal, and it's a great excuse to go out with my girls."

"Hell yeah, we're going to get a little crazy." I fist pump the air.

To be continued..

Made in the USA
Lexington, KY
12 November 2019